PROLOGUE

As they swept into the final bend the eight horses left in the race were closely bunched. They turned into the final straight, clods of the soft earth being thrown high, the brightly clothed riders crouched in the saddles, standing in the stirrups as the straining muscles of the powerful animals they rode drove hard for the finishing line. Two hundred yards out the leaders began to fade and Scarlet Emperor moved out of the group, smoothly, grey flanks gleaming with sweat, and from the stands came the slow; murmurous sound of excitement, a rising crescendo of noise from thousands of throats.

Whips flailed in the air in desperation but the big grey horse was now in the clear by a neck. The animal's stride seemed to lengthen as it drove hard for the line, nostrils flaring, hoofbeats thundering rhythmically, and the hysteria of the crowd enveloped the tiring horses, urging one final effort as they carried the wild hopes of the punters in the stands and along the finishing straight.

In the final hundred yards the result was beyond doubt: Scarlet Emperor was ahead by a length, thundering for the line, as cameras flashed above the enclosure and the ululations of the crowd hammered against the roof of the stand. The horses flashed past the finishing tape; men and women were on their feet, yelling, in excitement, derision and disappointment, and as the pack slowed, pulling up into a canter, and a veil of steam rose from the sweating horses the noise began to subside, the shouting fell away until there was only a low hum, the long swell of fading discussions, a murmuring of bees on the evening air.

The door to the private box was thrust open and the dark, stubble-haired Irishman came swaggering in, his features animated, his eyes glowing with pleasure and pride. He advanced towards the window, planted his hands on his lean hips and savoured the scene below in the paddock. 'Aaarh, a fine sight it was, to be sure. As soon as Scarlet Emperor took that last bend I knew it was all over for the others. A fine horse, a fine horse.'

The big man with the steel-grey eyes made no immediate response as he stood beside the Irishman, watching the scene impassively. His arms were folded across his broad chest. He was in his late forties now, the Irishman guessed: deep-set eyes, a mouth hard as iron, a scar reddening the line of his jaw; The knife that had done that had not been too far from the jugular, the Irishman considered: he wondered what had happened to the man who had wielded the weapon. Nothing good, he imagined. 'You'll not be a racing man, of course,' he said quietly.

The big man grunted dismissively, and shook his head. He glanced sideways at the Irishman. 'I believe that for some people it is an addiction. Is it that for you?'

The Irishman was aware once more of the man's heavy accent; the English was slow though almost perfect, but the intonation was clipped, marked with its foreign origin. He hesitated, then shrugged. 'Well, 'tis well enough known, that for the Irish racing is in the blood, and the Curragh comes second only to Holy Mother Church, but 'tis for me only a pleasure, the kind of brief rush of excitement, the surge in the blood that makes life worth living.' He glanced slyly at his companion. 'Like taking pleasure with a woman when she resists.'

The cold, hard eyes flickered briefly in his direction. There was a hint of contempt in the glance. He folded his arms over his broad chest. 'The surge of excitement that you speak of, it can be achieved in many ways. Horses, women, violence, deceit . . . each man will have his own particular form of pleasure. This horse now, this Scarlet Emperor, you are pleased not only because it won a certain sum of money for you. I believe there is the added pleasure of knowing that you have deceived . . .' A hand made a brief, contemptuous gesture towards the crowds in the enclosure below. 'To deceive all those people, for you that is more of the thrill, is it not?'

The Irishman grinned, ducked his head in admission. 'The fact that many of them have been conned? You're right, of course.'

'What is the real identity of that animal?' There was no real curiosity in the man's tone.

The Irishman bared his teeth in a grimace. 'Ah, well, now what's in a name? Sure enough, we've run him a few times in Ireland, held him back, so we could allow the handicappers to take a view of him. But the races he did win, well, they were under the name Orient Pearl. But it's a game, you see, it's a matter of outwitting those who'd be trying to outwit you. You know, there's a lot of checks they make these days: saliva, DNA, profiling — it's not like a hundred years ago when they could only go by the sight of an animal, or get the horse-doctors to check its teeth and that sort of thing. Nowadays, the things you have to do to avoid the inspections . . .'

He realised, when the man glanced at him, that there was a complete lack of interest in his companion's eyes. He was a hard man, this one. His voice died away. The two men stood there in silence for a little while, watching the seething crowd below. When the door to the private box opened and the sandy-haired man came in, grinning broadly, the Irishman turned towards him. 'Well, me friend, did you get the money on?'

Toddy Cleaver punched the air in a triumphant gesture. 'Too damn right! The team managed to get most of the bets down.'

'What was the starting price like?'

The sandy-haired man exposed his crooked teeth in a wide grin. 'Better than expected, in fact. We got three to one, and there doesn't seem to have been a whisper out about Scarlet Emperor. So am I a fixer, or am I not?'

The crowing speaker was only a little above medium height; his sandy hair was thinning even at the age of thirty, but his eyebrows were bushy, his complexion fair, and his features were notable for the open-faced innocence he was able to assume. The backs of his hands were freckled, his thick fingers seemingly clumsy. There was about him a certain infectious, friendly air that had done much to assist him in his criminal activities along the Tyne. The marks were easily conned; even some of the hard men in the criminal fraternity were sometimes unsure about him, though common sense made them wary of any dealings with him. And it was well known that the boyish air also concealed a ruthlessness in Toddy Cleaver that had from time to time exploded into violence.

The cocky jubilation had clearly been an irritation to the man who had been waiting in the private box. 'You will recall, I hope, that I am not here to watch horses race.' There was a grating tone in the voice; his indifferent gaze had turned away from the window and he was staring at them. The Irishman hesitated, glanced at his companion and waited. This was not his affair: it was a sideshow as far as he was concerned, although he was aware that for some reason it was a matter of importance to the development of a closer relationship between the three of them. He recognised that it was something that had to be done before there could be any real commitment to the impending arrangements they were planning. When the request had been made by the big man, the Irishman suspected it had been by way of a test. A proving ground for Toddy Cleaver. He could have done the job himself, of course, and efficiently, without asking any questions, but maybe the grey-eyed man knew that well enough, and had chosen to give the task to Toddy Cleaver. He wanted to test the man's mettle. It was like a matter of good faith.

The sandy-haired fixer moved forward quickly, unslung the binoculars from his neck and handed them to his questioner. 'Use these, you'll get a better view: concentrate on that bookie's box, down there near the finishing line. You see the bookie's board? Honest Lenny Logan, that's the one.' Toddy Cleaver stood beside the man with the cold eyes, eagerly scanning the crowd himself. He grinned. 'Huh. Lenny Logan is as crooked as they come, but that's no matter. Now there, you see the man we're talking about? The one you wanted me to sort out? Just watch . . . he's there right now, at the edge of that group at Lenny's pitch.'

Curiously, the Irishman moved closer to stand beside the other two men at the window: after a moment he caught sight of the target, a thickset, burly man, heavy-shouldered, but one who would no doubt move lightly on his feet. He was standing with his arms folded, a stillness among the swirl of men moving around him, as though he was waiting for something.

'I hope you realise,' Toddy Cleaver muttered, 'I'm giving up one of my own here.'

As they watched, the Irishman became aware of another man, short, denim-jacketed, edgy in his movements, working his way towards the target. There was no meeting of eyes as he brushed past him, but there was a brief glimpse of a touching, a movement of hands, but the target remained impassive.

'That's it; that's the first step,' the sandy-haired man approved. 'Now, any moment now, we'll see . . .'

The target unfolded his arms and one hand reached down towards his side. There was a hesitation, and then he stiffened, touched the pocket where the drop had been made. For one moment he remained absolutely still; then immediately he had begun to move. He turned his head, glanced about him, then stepped away from Honest Lenny Logan's pitch. The crowd milled about him, men tearing up tickets, others queueing to collect their winnings from the course bookmakers and the Tote. The target began to shoulder his way towards the stands. As he did so the Irishman caught sight of other movements in the crowd, not aimless but purposeful, three men ploughing their way through the crowd, converging on the target. From the height of the private box, looking down towards the paddock, it was possible to identify the deliberate nature of the movements, the target moving away, three other dark-clothed men striding forward in a pincer movement.

Toddy Cleaver scratched his sandy hair and chuckled gleefully. 'Here we go. Just like I set it all up. The boys are making the hit.'

The big man beside him still had the binoculars trained on the scene. All three men in the private box watched as the target was approached. The first of the trackers put out a hand, touched the target on the arm. The target turned, swung around to face the man who had touched him then backed away, a certain urgency in his movements. The other two pursuers moved in on him and he pushed against the crowd, tried to break into a run. He flailed his arms, tried to thrust away from the men seeking to detain him, dart through the thinning crowd that surged about him. But he was now held by one arm; he swung a fist and immediately there was a struggle as the three trackers moved in close with a flurry of arms and legs. A woman screamed, a man fell, and people scattered from the fighting group. But the target was no match for three men; he struggled, kicking for a few moments, but then almost fatalistically gave up; he was on his knees, held in an armlock, and he raised his free hand in submission. The crowd hesitated, men moving back to gawp in curiosity, standing around as the target was dragged to his feet. One of the pursuers waved his hands, shouting, ordering people to stand clear, then the small group moved away, the target restrained, pushed towards the exit.

'Neat, and sweet and clean,' the man with the sandy hair purred. 'Did I not say I'm a fixer?'

The binoculars were handed back to him silently as the big man turned away from the window; When his eyes fixed on Cleaver, his glance was contemptuous, unimpressed. 'Tell me exactly, what is it I have just witnessed?'

Toddy Cleaver's cockiness was quickly deflated, and his eyes widened. He glanced briefly at the Irishman, then back to his interrogator. 'I did it. I arranged things, like you asked. You said I was to get that guy sorted, and quietly. I did that, but sweet as a nut.' There was a hint of nervousness in his grin. 'Hey, I know you wouldn't want to be tied up in anything, any more than I would, or our Mick friend here for that matter. So if you wanted the target sorted, that's fine, but I played it clever. I used a few contacts, passed on some information.' He was regaining his confidence, glowing in self-satisfaction, his boyish face lit up, his chest swelling with pride. 'Why do the job ourselves? I asked meself. Keep our own hands clean. You want that guy sorted? Let the fuzz do it for us. That guy will be out of circulation for quite a while, is my guess. It's my loss, as I said, because he was one of mine, but hey — if you want him sorted, I'm your man.' There was a short silence. Puzzled, the sandy-haired man grew uncomfortable, shuffled in uncertainty. 'So, what's with the long face?'

'You are telling me that those men were police?' the big man grated.

Toddy Cleaver bit his lip, frowned and nodded. 'Well, yeah, and they'll put him away. Get him out of your hair, like you asked. He'll be charged with possession. He's got a record already, far as I can make out, so he'll be inside for a while. And we can get on with our business. Isn't that the point of all this? You asked me to get him dealt with. I did just that, even though you didn't say nothin' about why you wanted him out of the way. I mean, what was the problem with this guy anyway? Who was he to you?'

There was no relaxation in the hard mouth. 'That is not your affair. But you've brought in the police. I think that was unwise. It brings in complications. It could give rise to further problems. I hope that will not be so. But bringing them in . . .' He made a sound of displeasure, deep in his throat. He stood squarely in front of the sandy-haired man, staring at him in cold contemplation for a little while. At last, with a dissatisfied curl of his lip he grunted and brushed past his two companions, making his way towards the door of the box.

For a moment the Irishman went cold: he had the gnawing feeling the deal would be off.

But at the doorway the big man paused, thoughtfully, glanced back, noted the anxious perspiration that had gathered on the brow of the sandy-haired man, the tension that was apparent in the line of the Irishman's lean body. His reluctance was apparent as he nodded in slow decision. 'All right. I will take the matter on trust: this is your country, not mine, your police, your contacts. I am less than happy, but . . . we will proceed as planned. The contract will go ahead. Arrangements can now be put in place. But . . .' His lips drew back almost in a snarl as he grimaced with distaste. He pointed a menacing finger in Toddy Cleaver's direction. 'When I asked you to deal with this man, this was not an outcome I had been expecting. Perhaps I did not make myself clear at the time. So I must give you the benefit of the doubt.' He put his hand on the door handle, took a deep breath and glared stonily at the two men standing silently facing him. 'It is not how I anticipated the matter to have been brought to a conclusion. In the East, it was our custom and practice to deal with such matters more effectively.' His glance was icy. 'With *permanence.*'

CHAPTER 1

Detective Chief Inspector Charlie Spate was not a man given to brooding introspectively. In his own view he lived a life that was relatively ordered in nature. He found his work congenial: it was nothing to do with the protection of the public or the maintenance of standards of public morality. He just liked catching villains. And he was not particularly concerned about the methods he occasionally used to achieve a successful collar. It wasn't a game he was in. There were real people out there in the street, people who enjoyed violence, sometimes merely for its own sake. There were fraudsters and thieves, killers and conmen, wheeler-dealers and controllers and hitmen. It was his job to put them away. He achieved job satisfaction from doing just that.

He knew he had the reputation of being a loner, but that was almost inevitable because of the scuttlebutt that went around the headquarters, not least because of the baggage he had brought with him. The purge that had taken place a few years ago in the Met had resulted in a shakeout of officers: he had been one of those who had escaped suspension, but who had been advised that a move out of the Met would be advisable. For the good of the service, as they said. He had found a certain wry amusement in that phrase. What they really meant was that they found him — his use of contacts, his methods, the kind of pressure he sometimes put on villains, the range of deals he made to attain his objectives — they found him an embarrassment. Exposing him to the Press hadn't been an option: details might have emerged which could lead to other heads rolling, from more senior positions. So a quiet discussion; some measured advice, backed by hinted threats, and a move north had been arranged.

But what they hadn't quite understood, either in the Met or here in the north, was that a leopard didn't change his spots overnight. And Charlie had desires that required satisfaction. Villain-catching wasn't the only thing that brought him pleasure. So it was Elaine Start he really blamed for the predicament he now found himself in, Detective Sergeant Elaine Start. Even the thought of her now stirred him. He couldn't quite understand why he was so obsessed with her. It could have been merely the fact that they worked closely together from time to time; it could have been her body, the thought of which was a constant temptation. She was a good-looking woman, but she could not be described as particularly beautiful. She had a sharp tongue. She wasn't above putting him down severely, in spite of the difference in rank, particularly if he crossed the line she had drawn. He was sapient enough, and possessed sufficient self-knowledge to guess that part of the problem was that she maintained her distance, resisted his advances with a cool politeness, and yet from time to time seemed to be dropping hints that at the right place, and at the right time, things could be more promising.

Or maybe it was just that she presented a real challenge to his male ego, and his lust was a response to that challenge. She represented a fortification he burned to breach.

So in a sense, she was at least partly to blame. In an indirect way.

Gloomily he thrust thoughts of Elaine Start from his mind, shrugged into his jacket and headed for the door, towards one of those occasions he hated most of all: a meeting in the briefing room, chaired by that smooth bastard Assistant Chief Constable Jim Charteris.

Charlie Spate didn't like Charteris and made little secret of it. The ACC was an ambitious man who would be spending no longer than he had to on Tyneside. There was every evidence that he regarded himself as superior to his colleagues; he trusted no one, made sure that he took credit both where it was due and also where it was not, and was always on the lookout for an advantage. Charteris had his eyes set on distant horizons but that didn't mean he failed to pick up detail, and he was always using people in pursuit of his own objectives. And Charlie was clear what those objectives were: self-aggrandisement, self-promotion, clawing up the greasy pole to the top. Charlie had no doubt Charteris would make it, come hell, high water, storm or flood.

And he had the sneaking, irritating suspicion that Charteris might even find some way to take Elaine Start with him.

Charlie nodded to her as he entered the briefing room. She sat there straight-backed, flanked by two other officers. She regarded him coolly, a little speculatively, as though she was seeing him for the first time. He wondered whether the rumours had reached her: he glared at the other two officers seated beside her. If either of those two bastards opened their mouths he'd string their entrails to a barbed wire fence. And yet, reason prevailed, he didn't think either of them would have known, could have known, where he had got the information from. And yet someone did, for he was aware there were whispers . . .

The Assistant Chief Constable was entering the room as Charlie took his seat. He came in as though marching onto a parade ground, immaculately uniformed, his greying hair carefully combed, a thick file tucked under his left arm. He glanced around at the waiting officers, nodded, took the seat at the head of the table facing the small group, settled himself, opened the file and began to read its contents silently. Several minutes passed.

Charlie knew the ACC would have read the file earlier. This was just a way of exerting a little pressure, confirming his control of events. Charlie folded his arms and glanced sideways to Elaine Start: she remained staring straight ahead. She was on her best behaviour.

At last Charteris grunted, leaned back in his chair and looked at each of the officers in turn. 'Dieter Barschel,' he said.

Charlie licked his dry lips. Charteris had held his glance on Charlie, finally.

'The hearing begins tomorrow,' Charteris announced.

'That's right, sir,' Charlie replied.

'We will of course get a conviction.'

It was a statement, but it held an underlying question. 'The Crown Prosecution Service lawyers are fairly confident for once,' Charlie suggested. 'They haven't raised any particular difficulties. It's an open and shut case; we got Barschel bang to rights—'

'I admire your originality of phrase,' Charteris cut in coldly, drumming his elegant fingers on the file in front of him, 'but I assume the CPS has had access to all the facts?'

Stiffly, Charlie remarked, 'We've given them all the facts at our disposal; they've gone through the file; we've had a couple of case conferences—'

'*All* the facts, DCI?'

Charlie glared at his superior officer. Doubt gnawed at his mind again; he didn't know how much Charteris knew, or was niggling for. 'I don't understand what you mean, sir.'

Charteris was silent for a little while, stroking his lower lip thoughtfully, but he kept his eyes fixed on Charlie. At last he commented, 'It's just that there are a few elements in this case that I'm uncertain about. I mean, it's a bit unusual, is it not?'

Charlie hated the clipped manner in which the ACC spoke. 'Unusual, sir? I don't follow you. It was a simple arrest. We caught Barschel in possession. It's all straightforward.'

'Hardly that,' Charteris insisted, smiling without warmth. 'I don't recall any other instance in my career where the evidence is *so* . . . overwhelming.'

'That's a bad thing, sir?' Charlie asked, unable to keep the sarcasm out of his tone.

Charteris raised an eyebrow. 'It's like an over-egged pudding, DCI, too rich to stomach comfortably. How often have we ever caught a villain who is not only in possession of drugs, but is also carrying counterfeit money?'

Charlie felt the blood drain from his cheeks. He sat bolt upright. He was aware of Elaine Start turning her head to look at him. Charlie cleared his throat. 'I don't understand, sir.'

There was a certain bland indifference in the ACC's tone. 'As officer in charge of the case you should have been aware of all the facts. The CPS have agreed that Barschel can be charged with possession of a prohibited drug, cocaine to be exact. But you didn't take the money into consideration?'

Flustered, Charlie protested, 'We found a lot of money on him, and it's to be used in evidence, as support for the charge that he was not just in possession but he was dealing as well.'

'Of course,' Charteris commented with dangerous mildness, 'he could have won the money on the nags.'

'He wasn't observed making any bets,' Charlie protested, 'and anyway . . .' His voice died away as he glared at the ACC. He had the feeling he was being hoisted out to dry. 'This is the first time I've heard that the money we took from him was funny stuff.'

Charteris shrugged. 'It's only recently been confirmed. The notes are extremely good forgeries. When I received the information, I immediately took counsel with the Chief Constable. We were in agreement. Because of other issues arising, in Barschel's trial we won't be using the fact that the notes were counterfeit. Not in court. We'll stick to the drugs charge. But it raises questions, doesn't it?'

There was a long silence in the room. Beads of perspiration touched Charlie's lips. He waited. He hoped his suspicions were ill-based; he hoped the questions were not to be directed to him.

'Who will be presenting the evidence?' Charteris asked in a silky tone.

Charlie glanced towards one of the officers seated beside Elaine Start. 'It was DS Adams who made the collar, along with two other officers, so it's appropriate that he should be presenting—'

'I don't think so,' Charteris cut in coldly. 'I understand that you were the officer in charge.'

Charlie took a deep breath. 'Yes, but—'

'And it was you who ordered the initial surveillance, wasn't it?' Charteris persisted.

Charlie felt a cold knot form in his stomach. He glanced sideways towards Elaine Start; there was an odd expression in her eyes as their glances locked. She *had* heard the bloody rumours. 'I ordered it sir, yes, but since I didn't actually take part in the operation—'

'You see, DCI,' Charteris cut in once more, 'there's a bit of a problem if any officer other than yourself takes the witness stand. The arresting officers, well, they could be asked questions they wouldn't be able to answer. I would suspect, for instance, that none of the officers in this room have any idea how you came by the information that resulted in you ordering the surveillance and the subsequent arrest.' He paused, raised his eyebrows in mock innocence and looked at the two men and the woman facing him. They all remained silent, and still. 'So there's the problem,' Charteris continued. 'They wouldn't be able to answer that question, or certain others.'

Charlie hands were damp; he rubbed his palms on his thighs. He felt cold, but there was a surge of anger in his veins. He remained silent, waiting.

'For instance,' Charteris went on, 'it would seem the defence has requested certain items of CCTV coverage from the race track. I wonder . . . just what will that show; DCI Spate?'

Puzzled, Charlie merely glowered.

'I take it that none of the officers actually approached Barschel before the . . . ah . . . arrest?' Charteris asked, glancing away from Charlie.

Detective Sergeant Adams cleared his throat nervously. 'No, sir. We were under specific instructions, sir.'

Charteris raised an eyebrow, nodded. 'Quite so.' He turned back to Charlie. 'And your reasons for ordering surveillance on Barschel, they were soundly based, DCI?'

'I had no reason to doubt my informant,' Charlie growled sullenly. 'I was told he'd be carrying; I was told he was a dealer.'

'So it was a paid informant, then?' Charteris leaned forward, his slim, predatory fingers now still on the file cover in front of him. 'Are we to be privileged to learn the identity of this informant?'

Charlie licked his lips. He'd been stupid, he knew that now.

But his stupidity had to come to an end. 'I'd rather not say at this stage, sir. But my informant has given me reliable information in the past.'

The lie had come easily to his lips, but Charteris was clearly not about to pursue the matter. Instead the assistant chief constable gave an exaggerated sigh and raised his hands dismissively. 'Well, you see the problem clearly enough, I imagine. We can't expect an unbriefed officer to present the evidence when he doesn't know the full background. It's got to be you, DCI Spate. It's up to you to take the stand, and give such evidence as you consider necessary to obtain a conviction.'

'I don't understand!' Charlie burst out angrily. 'This is only a preliminary hearing! It's a bloody formality. It'll be over in half an hour — we'll make the charges, get some evidence admitted, and Barschel will be bound over for trial. It'll be a few months before it comes up to the High Court but we'll oppose bail because of the nature of the offence. We'll argue that we believe Barschel will attempt to scarper, jump bail, or that he'll interfere with other witnesses, the usual stuff—'

'Ah, but that's the problem, DCI,' Charteris interrupted smoothly. He appeared to be enjoying Charlie's discomfiture. 'It's questionable whether the defence will indeed request bail. What exactly do we know about this man Dieter Barschel?'

Sullenly, Charlie answered, 'He's Romanian by birth. But he moved to Germany, then Italy twenty years ago: it seems he was a footballer, and at one stage was set for big things. Real Madrid took him on loan from Roma it seems—'

'I'm not a football fan, myself,' Charteris murmured.

'He ended up playing briefly for Newcastle United, then slipped to non-league football in Durham after he suffered some bad fractures of his left leg. Like most of those players he hadn't spent his money wisely and he was down on his uppers after a few years. That's when he drifted into crime—'

'Not exactly a big player, was he?' Charteris commented. 'On the crime scene, I mean.' He opened the file in front of him, glanced at it. 'A little bit of larceny; stealing a car; couple of pub fights. He's been a bit of a layabout since he finished playing football but he's never been a Professor Moriarty, has he? Never a Napoleon of crime. But suddenly, out of the blue, when he's no history that we're aware of, you put three men on him at the racetrack and bingo! You pull him in on a charge of possession. I can imagine which way the defence is going to play things. Particularly if they found something on CCTV, as they seem to have.' He grimaced sourly. 'The fact is, DCI Spate, I have my own sources of information. And my little bird tells me the preliminary hearing is not going to be the cakewalk you seem to think it might be. The signs are pointing to an argument from the defence that Dieter Barschel has no case to answer.'

'That's ridiculous!' Charlie burst out angrily.

'In whose judgement?' Charteris snapped. 'The fact is, there are likely to be questions raised which can only be sensibly answered by you. So the other officer can stand down. And you, DCI Spate, will be presenting the evidence against this man Barschel. I just hope to God you've got the answers. The Chief Constable won't look kindly to a claim from the defence, arguing it's a matter of unlawful arrest!'

Charlie sat up very straight, aware that the others weren't looking at him. His mind was spinning. There was something wrong in all this: the Barschel arrest had always been seen by him as a straightforward collar, of no great significance, even if the reasons for it had never been quite as simple as they seemed. But he was puzzled. He felt he was missing something; there was a wild card in the deck that he didn't know about. Charteris was keeping something to himself, setting Charlie up for some reason he was unable to comprehend. And the problem was Charlie had something to hide.

Elaine Start was leaning forward in her chair. 'There's something I don't quite understand, sir.'

ACC Jim Charteris looked at her and smiled slightly. His voice was soft. 'And just what would that be, DS Start?'

Charlie hated him.

'It's the matter of this money Dieter Barschel was carrying. You say that the experts who have been consulted now conclude that the money is counterfeit. And you . . . well . . . you imply that the case against Barschel for drug dealing might not hold up. At least, that's what . . .' Her voice died away as she shot a ragged glance in Charlie's direction.

'Go on, DS Start,' Charteris urged quietly.

'Well, sir, if the current case against Barschel is a bit, well, weak or open to challenge on the drugs thing, why don't we strengthen the case by making use of the counterfeit notes? In the end, we'll get what we want . . . or stand a better chance of getting Barschel, if we get him on both counts.'

Charteris smiled indulgently. 'A good point, DS Start. But unfortunately, life is never that simple, in reality. I've discussed the matter with the chief constable, and we've had a few meetings with neighbouring forces. What's become apparent is that we have a widespread problem on our hands. A task force in Middlesbrough have been working on the matter for eighteen months, and they think they're close to finding the source of this funny money in Cleveland. But discovering the notes on Dieter Barschel . . . well, it now seems the matter has spread like a virus to us here on the Tyne as well. It's become apparent that one of the methods used by the gang — and it seems it's a gang of some skill in the printing of the paper — is laundering the counterfeit notes at the racetracks in the north. As we're all aware, a lot of cash transactions take place at these events, and a number of people have been under surveillance at York and other places. Not, of course, at Newcastle and not, to my knowledge, our Mr Dieter Barschel.'

His eyes swivelled towards Charlie and their gazes locked for a long moment. 'So the problem is that while our friends in Cleveland are well on with their investigations, we've unfortunately been caught by surprise. Inter-force cooperation is not always what one would wish it to be. However . . .'

'Are you suggesting, sir, that if we add the charge of passing counterfeit notes on Dieter Barschel,' Elaine Start said quietly, 'we might prejudice an ongoing investigation into the counterfeiting gang?'

Charteris smiled in encouragement at her perspicacity. 'Well, ongoing as from now. Yes, you make the point precisely. And if you come to my office after this meeting I will brief you on the matter.'

'Sir?'

'It's been decided that you will be heading up the team that will be liaising with the Cleveland task force. You will be working the Newcastle end of things, while DCI Spate confines his activities to other matters.'

Charlie felt a rage burning inside him. He glared at ACC Charteris, who seemed cynically pleased about something.

'Anyway, DCI Spate, I'll let you have this file on Barschel. It doesn't really include anything you don't have — or should have, at least. But it's as well to have everything at your fingertips. Meanwhile,' he added, almost pleasantly, 'I wish you luck at the preliminary hearing tomorrow.'

As Charteris strode from the room, with Elaine Start following him, Charlie closed his eyes. He sat still for several minutes; he was enveloped in that close, warm darkness again, there was soft flesh under his hands, there was a body writhing urgently under his and a voice murmuring in his ear.

'Charlie, there's something you could do to help me . . .'

He opened his eyes. He heard a scraping of chairs, the others leaving. He looked around: as she was leaving the room Elaine Start cast a quick glance behind her. He could see puzzlement in her eyes.

Stupid. He'd been incredibly stupid.

CHAPTER 2

Eric Ward finished his cup of coffee in the police canteen and made his way down to the cells. A constable accompanied him to unlock the first cell door: Eric's client sat huddled in a corner, elbows on his knees, a sullen look on his face. Eric observed him silently for a few moments. The man was in his forties now; and the lean muscle he had used to explode through defences twenty years ago had gone: he was heavy-bodied, still light on his feet, but sagging around the waist. His features were mottled and his attitude sullen; discontent had etched lines around his mouth and his pouched eyes.

Out of curiosity, Eric had obtained from the Newcastle Library archives some old film of matches played by Newcastle United, in which Dieter Barschel had played a part. There had been a few shots of the younger man, now almost unrecognisable in build. The man himself had had little to say about the old days, when, trying to put him at ease, Eric had asked about his past life. He had been somewhat dismissive of those days, when success had come quickly to him. Perhaps it was the realisation that years of easy money had been negated by foolish frittering away of earnings at the racetrack, on women, and failed business ventures.

'There are always vultures,' he had muttered to Eric in reluctant explanation. 'They hover around with their greedy beaks open, waiting to tear at the flesh of your earnings.'

He had been similarly reluctant to talk about his earlier days, in Germany, Italy and Spain, and on his childhood he would not be drawn beyond saying that he had come from a poor family, and that it had not been easy to get out of Romania in the days of communism and dictatorship. 'It was football that got me out,' he admitted. 'I was signed to play for the junior team at Dynamo Berlin.'

Now, as Eric stood over him, he remained hunched in silent anger. It was an attitude he had retained ever since he had agreed that Eric should represent him: guilty or not, he was consumed with a bitterness that seemed to tear at his vitals. And at first he had given Eric very little to work with. He had seemed to regard his confinement, and the charges against him, as an irrelevance. Rather, he gave the appearance of concentrating upon other matters, frowning as he went over things inside his own head. He demonstrated a certain indifference to his incarceration, simply shook his head, denying the offence with which he was charged. It was only after Jackie Parton had arrived at Eric's office on the Quayside that things had begun to change.

Eric's secretary, Susie Cartwright, had been smiling when she announced the ex-jockey's arrival. Jackie Parton always had that effect upon her: somehow or other the wiry, wizened little man with the bowed legs always managed to bring a smile to her face even when she was at her most disapproving of Eric's client list and failure to deal sufficiently quickly with the files she regularly deposited on his desk. It was late in the afternoon when Jackie arrived and she was about to leave; Eric felt he had done enough for the day so when Parton came into the room he asked him if he would like to join him in a drink.

'Never say no to a snifter, Mr Ward,' Jackie had assured him.

Eric went into the back room and took the whisky bottle from the filing cabinet, along with two glasses. He suspected

Susie knew very well of its existence, but she had never mentioned it in spite of her general mothering of him: she knew he drank but sparely, because of the effect it could have. The medication he took against the effects of glaucoma kept the pain at bay, but problems could be exacerbated by an excess of alcohol. He poured two glasses, handed one to his visitor.

'Well, here's to you, bonny lad,' Jackie toasted, 'and confusion to your enemies.'

'About whom you've come to warn me?' Eric queried.

'Not exactly, not exactly,' the ex-jockey replied and sipped thoughtfully at the golden liquid in his glass tumbler.

Eric eyed him curiously. He had known Jackie Parton for some years. The man had made a living as a jockey and had gained for himself quite a reputation on Tyneside. Most of his racing had been in the north, at York, Ripon, Newcastle and Carlisle, but it had come quite suddenly to an end. Eric didn't know the full details and Jackie never talked about it, but he had been badly beaten in a dark alley and there were rumours that he'd refused to hold back a mare that had been favourite; there were counter rumours that he had in fact welshed on a contract, or had deliberately thrown a race on which some big money was riding. The truth of the matter never really emerged, but it had been the end of his career. Even so, he had never lost his popularity along the Tyne; he had a large number of contacts and although Eric was never quite sure how Jackie Parton actually made a living he had used him regularly over the years, to obtain information that might be useful to the clients he was serving. In fact, though the two men had never become intimates, moving as they did in entirely different circles, a certain friendship had developed between them. It had been somewhat strained when Eric and his wife Anne had divorced, because Jackie Parton had considerable regard for Anne and felt that the separation, and consequent divorce, had largely been Eric's fault. But the disagreement had since been papered over and their relationship had been re-established, albeit on a slightly less easy basis. But Eric had been surprised to find the ex-jockey coming unannounced to his office: it was the first time it had happened, because generally they would meet only when Eric had requested some assistance.

Eric leaned back in his chair. 'So, if it's not a warning, well, I'm happy enough to see you, Jackie, but is it business? You wanting to renegotiate the retainer I pay you?'

For a moment Eric thought he had offended his visitor but Jackie shook his head vigorously. 'Naw, nothin' like that Mr Ward. I'm happy with what I get. Fact is, I thought I'd pop around to see you, have a little chat when I heard about this case you got comin' up.'

'Dieter Barschel? The ex-footballer?'

Jackie Parton nodded. 'Aye, that's right. Seen him play a few times, in the old days. Used his muscle a bit; the Toon Army loved him. Like the old style of centre forward some reckoned. Hard and direct, but not lacking in skill either. He came on loan from a Spanish club, after he played in Italy for a few years, but really he was a bit on the skids, and he got into a few fights. The terraces, the Leazes End, they loved that, mind.'

'I didn't know you were a supporter.'

Jackie smiled, shrugged diffidently. 'Aye, well, you had to be if you hung around the Newcastle area. And after I finished on the racetrack, well, I used to go to Gallowgate from time to time, though that was after Barschel had finished really. It was his own fault, you knaa: he went in for the tackle and shattered his femur. It ended him. He had two seasons after that, non-league, but he was never the same player.'

'So what's your interest in him now?' Eric asked.

Jackie Parton sipped reflectively at his whisky, put his elbows on his knees and leaned forward. He shook his head with an abstracted air. 'When I heard that Barschel had been collared, and got to know the charges, well, I got to thinking: things wasn't kind of makin' sense, you know what I mean? And as it happened, I was at the racetrack that day when it all went down.'

Eric frowned. 'When Barschel was arrested?'

Jackie nodded. 'It was the day that Scarlet Emperor came in at three to one. And I could tell you a bit about that as well. If that nag was anything but a ringer, I'll take a runnin' jump into the Tyne. I'd keep my mouth closed mind, and wouldn't shout for help.' He grinned at the thought, shook his head. 'River's a lot cleaner than the old days, so old jokes aren't what they used to be. But Dieter Barschel: I saw what happened.'

'His arrest?' Eric queried, interested.

'That's right. Thing is, Mr Ward, it's a funny fact that when you get used to a place you can get a feeling if something is sort of . . . out of kilter, you know what I mean? When you go to the racetrack as often as I do you notice things. Sometimes it's a feeling of tension in the air; sometimes you feel a tingling, as though there's something about to happen that you can't put your finger on. It was like that, the day Barschel got took. It's nothing you can be certain of, but I wasn't alone in feelin' it. Couple of the fellers told me the same: they knew something was up. There were faces in the crowd, faces that didn't fit.'

'People you recognised, you mean?'

'Villains, no, not exactly. But when the polis is minglin', well, somehow the word gets around. A lot of people felt the atmosphere even though nothin' much was said. But people knew the polis was around. And then when I saw them going in on him, on Dieter Barschel, I said to myself, wey hey, bonny lad, what's aboot here?'

Eric watched the ex-jockey for a little while as he reflected upon the matter. 'What did you think was going on?'

Jackie Parton shrugged his lean shoulders. 'Something unusual. You see, Mr Ward, you get to know people, and you'll remember what it was like when you was working the streets, in the old days when you was on the beat. You didn't go for the small fry unless they was involved in something; a lot of the petty crime slips past because it's not worth polis time dealing with it. And Dieter Barschel was small-time.'

'He has a police record,' Eric murmured.

'Yeah, but not exactly long as your arm and heavy as lead. Dieter did his little bits of business, but it was all just earnin' a living, you know what I mean? He was a hard man on the football pitch, but he never had a reputation for putting the boot in anywhere else. But suddenly there he is at the racetrack, mindin' his own business, probably grafting at something or other — and I've picked up a few rumours about that as well — but it seems he was under surveillance by several coppers. Now that's a bit hard on a grafter like Dieter Barschel. I mean what did he do to deserve that?'

'I don't understand. Why are you surprised he was under surveillance?'

'Three plainclothes men watching a small-time grafter like Barschel? It's not canny, Mr Ward. It's a misuse of polis resources.'

Eric smiled slightly at the indignation in Parton's voice. 'The charge is that he was in possession of Class A drugs. Isn't that serious enough?'

Jackie shook his head. 'But that's another thing. There's been no chat along the river that'd suggest Barschel was dealing with the hard stuff. He might have been up to other things, but not drugs. He didn't have the connections. But there he is with three coppers on his tail, and at a specific moment they move in on him and nail him: not later, not earlier, but at that point just after Scarlet Emperor stole the race.'

'Opportunity . . .' Eric said slowly.

'No, there was a feeling something was up. I talked to a few of the racing lads down at the pubs: they all thought it was a bit queer, like. So I got curious like.' He regarded Eric owlishly for a few moments. 'You'll have a view of me, Mr Ward. I talk to villains; I listen to them; I give you information when you're looking for it. But the information I give you, well it concerns hard stuff, business I don't agree with. But if something is going down which I don't think is right, well, I don't like to see it.' He was silent for a little while, sipping his whisky. 'It got to me,' he said at last. 'So I talked to a few people, and went to see a feller I know.'

'And?'

'Well, he's the guy who processes some of the CCTV stuff that gets taken around about, and sure enough I was able to take a look at what happened that day. Saw meself struttin' around, large as life, but I wasn't up to any thin', of course. Other people were, but that's their business. But as far as Barschel was concerned, I looked at those tapes a lot, went over them several times, and I gradually began to get a picture, if you know what I mean, work out what I think was going on.'

Eric was curious. 'How do you mean?'

'It wasn't difficult to spot the fuzz.' Jackie smiled apologetically. 'It never is. You must have known that when you was on the beat in the back streets years ago, Mr Ward, before you got respectable.'

Eric laughed. 'I was aware that I didn't exactly merge into the background. So you spotted the plainclothes guys before they made the arrest?'

Jackie Parton grunted in contempt. 'Wasn't difficult. They didn't have a lot to do. Not interested in the racing. Just had eyes for one guy: Dieter Barschel.'

'Isn't that what surveillance is all about?' Eric queried. 'Yeah, but these coppers could have taken him at any point in time, discreetly, quietly. Instead they did it in one big rush. Why? Because they had to. They was waiting for something to happen. Something they knew was going to happen. Only then did they make their moves, and nail him.'

'What was the event they were waiting for?' Eric asked, intrigued.

'A drop. Something was handed to Barschel. To be more accurate, something was slipped into his pocket. And while I can't be sure, maybe he was expecting it because he didn't move at first, but it looked as though things didn't feel right to him, and he got a bit startled and he tried to move away.'

'That's when the arrest took place . . . What about the man who approached Barschel?'

Jackie Parton finished his drink and shook his head. 'Nobody I knew. I seen him around, but don't know his name.' He hesitated, and then added, 'But there's some other talk been going up and down the river. Maybe there's something in it, maybe not. And the connection is slight, but who knows? I'm still making enquiries about that. But I thought I ought to come to see you, and share a few thoughts.'

'So what conclusions have you come to after all this?'

'Conclusions? I think it's pretty obvious. It's more than a guess: I reckon that Dieter Barschel was set up. And I've got a vague idea just who might have put the whole thing together.'

Dieter Barschel's first reaction when Eric had told him about the result of Jackie Parton's curiosity had been explosive. 'That slut!' he had snarled, and then made use of some of the more colourful expressions he must have acquired during his footballing days, delivered in a curious mixture of Geordie overlaid with elements of the Romanian accent he had never managed to eradicate. When he had calmed down Eric told him what he proposed to do, and Barschel had listened intently, nodding from time to time. But Eric had also received the impression that after that first burst of volcanic anger the man had stepped back mentally, and was only half listening to Eric as he spoke. It was as though he had withdrawn behind a glass wall: he heard, he understood, he agreed tactics, but at the same time his mind was elsewhere, churning something over, balancing options available to him, preparing himself for another scenario entirely. If so, it was not one that he was prepared to share with Eric. He had still not confided completely even now; as Eric stood in front of him in the cell.

'Is there anything *else* you want to talk to me about, anything you think can help us in this whole situation?' Eric asked. 'You're clear, what I propose to do may start a hornet's nest around our ears.'

Dieter Barschel had stared at him blankly, saying nothing. Eric nodded, sighed and gestured towards the door. 'It'll be time to go up to the courtroom.'

The earlier minor celebrity that Dieter Barschel had enjoyed when playing for Newcastle had ensured that news of his arrest had been prominently displayed in the newspapers so Eric was not surprised to find a considerable number of people in the courtroom. There was a scattering of greyer men whom he imagined were former supporters of the former player, and the major newspapers, both in the locality and from wider afield, were represented. Proceedings got under way smoothly under the magistracy of Colonel Vaughan, a pale-eyed, luxuriantly moustached ex-Army man who had been made a Justice of the Peace in his retirement and ran his court with a punctilious regard for formality: the charges were read out and a not guilty plea was entered.

The solicitor acting for the Crown Prosecution read out a summary of the evidence against Dieter Barschel. Eric knew him well enough: a solicitor called Anstruther, he was in his fifties and the doldrums of CPS work seemed to have dulled his edge somewhat. He seemed to be in a hurry to get things over so he could go elsewhere. Fishing, perhaps. His voice was metallic and toneless, his reading of his brief unmarked by cadences. Colonel Vaughan had a bored expression on his face, though from time to time he cocked a bushy, disapproving eyebrow when there was a murmur from the reporters in the courtroom.

When the prosecution evidence was completed the Vaughan eyebrow was cocked in Eric's direction. 'I presume you will be making an application for bail, Mr Ward?'

Eric rose to his feet. 'Not at this point, sir.'

Anstruther's attention had strayed. He rose also, fumbling with his papers. 'The prosecution strenuously wishes to oppose the granting of bail,' he announced. 'The charges against the accused are of a serious nature. We have strong evidence to suggest that should the accused be freed on his own recognisance there is every expectation that he would enlist aid and support in removing himself from the jurisdiction. Naturally, we would expect his passport to be confiscated but having regard to the criminal circles within which Mr Barschel moves the prosecution believes that he would not find it difficult to obtain false documentation. Furthermore, there is the danger that while on bail the accused may well interfere with witnesses that the prosecution intends to call; there is the further consideration that . . .'

Anstruther paused. He raised his head, suddenly aware that Colonel Vaughan was glaring at him from the bench. He glanced sideways at Eric, puzzled, knocked out of his stride.

The magistrate smiled grimly. 'Perhaps you were not paying attention, Mr Anstruther. The defence is not requesting bail.'

'At this stage,' Eric added firmly; Colonel Vaughan frowned. He was caught off balance, and he did not like the feeling. He leaned forward, beckoned to the clerk of the court, and had a brief whispered conversation with him. He leaned back in his seat, nodding. He fixed Eric with a glance that expressed his displeasure. 'The accused has pleaded not guilty to the charges so how do you now wish to proceed?'

Almost casually, Eric answered, 'We wish to make a submission, sir, that in respect of the charges entered into the court record there is no case to answer.'

Colonel Vaughan was silent for a few moments. His eyes were a very pale blue but there was an opacity about them which made him appear even more formidable in that it was difficult to know what he was thinking. Eric had appeared before the Colonel previously: he had long held the view that in fact Colonel Vaughan thought about very little.

'I remind you, Mr Ward, that this is a preliminary hearing, the prosecution has presented its case, and it is normal for matters of . . . law . . . to be dealt with at the next hearing. In my experience, defence lawyers tend to wait until trial before they make such submissions. You must be aware that I cannot merely dismiss the prosecution case out of hand without hearing evidence for the defence. And in a case of such seriousness—'

'It is my intention to present evidence for the defence, sir,' Eric said.

A hint of colour appeared in the magistrate's face. He did not like to be interrupted: no one had dared do so during his days in the Army. 'Mr Ward,' he ground out, 'surely I need not remind you that by presenting your evidence now you will be displaying your hand, as they say, to the prosecution. It gives them that much more time to refute the case for the defence. In the best interests of your client—'

'I believe the best interests of my client will be served by the presenting of evidence to demonstrate there is no case to answer,' Eric insisted.

Colonel Vaughan bared his teeth, yellowing under his moustache. He wrinkled his nose in distaste and consulted again with the clerk of the court, then leaned back, fixing Eric with a glowering stare. 'Your submission is duly noted, since you won't listen to reason. How do you intend to present your evidence, so that a decision can be reached on this . . . preliminary matter?'

'I intend to call as a witness the arresting officer present at the racecourse when Mr Barschel was taken into custody.'

A light groan sounded deep in Colonel Vaughan's throat. There was a murmuring in the courtroom; Eric was aware of a general shuffling among the reporters. 'The arresting officer will presumably be called at the next hearing to give evidence for the prosecution,' Colonel Vaughan objected.

'At the trial, certainly,' Eric concurred. 'If the matter goes that far. For now, I would like to examine the man concerned.'

'This is not a matter that I can—'

'In the interests of justice,' Eric added.

Colonel Vaughan took a deep breath. He writhed in his seat, pulled at his moustache and glanced at Anstruther who was now fully awake, albeit somewhat nonplussed. 'Mr Anstruther, do you have anything to say on the matter?'

The CPS solicitor glanced around him, as though seeking guidance. 'This is somewhat unusual, I was not expecting . . .' He pulled himself together, looked back up to the bench. 'The arresting officer, he is not in court. In fact, it was not our intention to call him. Rather it was the intention of the prosecution to call as witness the officer who was in charge of the operation.'

Eric raised an eyebrow, smiled thinly at the CPS solicitor. 'Through the bench, may I ask who that officer may be?' Anstruther stared at him, remaining silent, thinking abstractedly. He was unhappy, caught unprepared .

'Mr Anstruther,' Colonel Vaughan rumbled in warning. The CPS lawyer shook himself. 'The officer in charge . . . it was Detective Chief Inspector Spate.'

'Mr Ward?' Colonel Vaughan queried. 'Up to you.'

Eric nodded in mock submission. 'Then I will call, to present evidence which I expect to be favourable to the defence, that particular officer: Detective Chief Inspector Charles Spate.'

CHAPTER 3

Charlie Spate's displeasure was evident in every line of his body as he made his way to the witness box. He managed to shoot one furious glance in Eric's direction as he passed him. The message was clear. This was not something that Charlie Spate would easily forget. The message carried further menace: Charlie Spate and Eric Ward had had dealings before, and though they had in the past reached agreed compromises in their relationship, from this point onwards all bets would be off. If Charlie Spate got his way, Eric Ward would pay dearly for this embarrassment.

Eric began quietly, speaking in a measured, even tone, taking the DCI through general matters such as his rank and recent promotion, his time on Tyneside, and his previous experience elsewhere, before turning to more serious matters in hand.

'At this stage, DCI Spate, I intend treating you as an officer friendly to the defence, in that I expect you to hold back no evidence which might arise in favour of my client.'

'That's understood,' Charlie Spate muttered.

'You'll also understand that if I feel my questions are not being honestly answered I will make application to the bench for permission to treat you as a hostile witness, and deal with you rather more . . . aggressively?'

Colonel Vaughan was displeased: the question smacked of an attack upon the integrity of the establishment and he was an Establishment man. 'I see no reason to take that tack at this stage, Mr Ward,' he snapped.

Eric smiled. 'A precaution on my part, sir. I was merely making the situation clear to the witness, so there should be no misunderstanding. So, DCI Spate, perhaps we should begin by referring to the day in question, when the arrest of my client was completed at the Newcastle racetrack. You will have received a full report of the actions taken from the arresting officers?'

'Of course. I received a written report from Detective Sergeant Adams, who was leading the team.'

'Perhaps you will tell the court exactly what happened on that occasion,' Eric suggested blandly.

Charlie Spate hunched forward, his hands gripping the wooden rail in front of him. He fixed his eyes on Eric: there was a malignant challenge in the glance that demonstrated he was not going to be trapped into any admissions, and that he would put every question Eric asked into a bank of reasons to extract revenge later, when the opportunity might present itself. 'As a result of information received,' he began coldly, 'I instructed three officers to be present that day at the racetrack in Newcastle. They were on general duty, but had been warned to keep an eye out for the accused, since it was suspected he was taking part in the dealing of prohibited substances.'

'Drugs,' Eric offered.

'That's right.'

'Had Mr Barschel ever previously come to your attention as a drug dealer?' Eric asked casually.

'He had a previous record; he was known to us—'

'As a drug dealer?'

DCI Spate hesitated for a moment. His eyes narrowed. 'Not specifically. But he was known to us.'

Eric Ward waved the point aside for the moment. 'Please continue.'

Charlie glanced sourly at the magistrate, but Colonel Vaughan's head was down as he took notes. There'd be no help there. 'The three officers I had detailed to the assignment took up their positions near a particular bookmaker's patch—'

'That would be Honest Lenny Logan's patch.'

Someone giggled in the courtroom and Colonel Vaughan raised his head, glaring.

'The officers kept the accused under surveillance for some twenty minutes,' Charlie Spate continued, 'as he moved around the enclosure. He—'

'During that time, was he behaving in a suspicious manner?' Eric interrupted.

Charlie Spate hesitated. 'The officers had their suspicions. They kept him in sight; followed him around. Then they finally observed that he was approached by another individual, some exchange took place and at that point they moved in to make an arrest.'

'On what grounds?'

Charlie's glance was hostile. 'He was suspected of receiving a packet.'

'And then — they . . . ?'

'They moved in to effect an arrest. The accused struggled, tried to run away but he was eventually subdued, arrested, and brought away from the track and—'

Eric raised a hand. 'Forgive me, just one moment . . . You say he was suspected of having received a packet. This was given to him by another man. Do you know the identity of that person?'

Charlie Spate hesitated. 'He was unknown to us.'

Eric allowed a degree of surprise to leak into his tone. 'No attempt was made to apprehend him?'

'No. He vanished in the crowd. The officers concentrated on Dieter Barschel.'

'Is that so?' Eric was silent for a few moments, watching Spate carefully. 'So after a package was passed to my client you arrested him but ignored the carrier . . . the facts you've just related to us consist of an accurate representation of events?'

Charlie shrugged. 'I didn't witness them personally, of course, but the notes of the arresting officers are agreed upon these facts, and the sequence in which they took place.'

Eric glanced up to the bench, engaged Colonel Vaughan with a wry smile, and said, 'So of course, we must take their word for what happened.'

Colonel Vaughan frowned, and shifted in his seat. He pursed his lips, not sure whether to take exception to the comment. Eric turned back to the DCI in the witness box. 'Are you aware that there are various security systems in place at the racetrack in question?'

'I am. It's common practice at meetings. The reasons are obvious.'

'Obvious, yes. So you are aware there is a CCTV system in operation at the track.'

'I am, yes.'

'Have you watched the footage that refers to the incidents you have just described?'

'I have.'

'How many times?' Eric asked quietly.

There was a slight hesitation before Spate replied. 'I've looked at it on several occasions.'

Eric consulted his notes. Casually, he asked, 'Having seen the footage several times, are you happy to accept the accuracy of the reports given to you by the arresting officers?'

Charlie Spate replied in a monotone. 'I have no reason to doubt the arresting officers. Detective Sergeant Adams and the men he led are officers of integrity and experience.' He looked directly at Eric. 'As are *most* officers in my experience — present and *past.*'

The inference was not lost to Eric. He knew well enough there were men in the force who regarded him as a traitor: he had been one of them, and now he was to be found on the other side, defending criminals who deserved to be put away, cross-questioning men with whom he had once worked, casting doubts on their honesty and integrity. He regarded the DCI calmly. 'All sorts of inferences can be drawn from watching footage of that kind,' he suggested. 'I also have had the opportunity to look closely at the tapes. You say that the person who is suspected of having delivered a package to Mr Barschel is not known to the police?'

'That's right.'

'And he vanished into the crowd.'

'Correct.'

'And no attempt was made to chase him, arrest that man?' Eric pressed.

Charlie Spate shook his head. 'They nailed Barschel. The other man escaped.'

'Hmmm. Escaped. As I said a moment ago, various interpretations are possible when footage of this kind is inspected closely. But some things will be irrefutable. Such as the fact that the man who you say delivered the package did not actually vanish into the crowd. The so-called delivery, the slipping of a package into my client's pocket, can be seen clearly . . . as also can the same man be seen, standing not ten feet away from the arresting officers when they struggle with my client and subdue him violently. Indeed, an interpretation of the scene might even lead one to suggest that the man you failed to apprehend, failed to arrest because he *escaped,* in your words, was in fact somehow *involved* in the arrest.'

'I don't know what you mean,' Charlie Spate replied woodenly. 'Is that a question?'

'If you wish,' Eric replied calmly. 'Was this man involved in the arrest?'

'That's ridiculous.'

'Your reply doesn't answer the question,' Eric responded. 'Was the man whose identity was not known to you still there, hanging around the fringe of the action, watching the arrest? Was he there, ensuring that the right man was apprehended . . . or maybe making sure that if Dieter Barschel looked like losing himself in the crowd there might be another pair of eyes available to direct the arresting officers into his path?

Was this mysterious individual not working with the police? In other words, was he a plant?'

Colonel Vaughan cleared his throat. 'Mr Ward,' he grumbled, 'you mentioned earlier that DCI Spate is not a hostile witness. Your questioning is more suited to a cross-examination. I'm not happy with it.'

Eric inclined his head. Charlie Spate spoke out firmly. 'The man we're talking about was not involved in the arrest.'

Eric smiled. 'I think others might disagree. From the tape, other interpretations are . . . possible. But let's move on.' He paused. 'We have — on my interpretation of the tape — a direct surveillance of Dieter Barschel, admittedly a petty criminal, by three officers who presumably were drawn from other, quite important duties. They spend a considerable time observing my client who, incidentally, does not move around according to the evidence of the CCTV footage, but remains in one position near the location of the bookmaker. Concentrating, in other words, on the results of the race, in which he had an interest, having placed a bet, with the aforesaid Honest Lenny Logan. Again, my view of the CCTV footage shows that this mysterious, unknown other man brushes against him, and a few seconds later my client appears disturbed, moves away — and the intrepid officers spring into action.'

'Mr Ward,' Colonel Vaughan pronounced with more than a hint of anger in his tone. 'That's not a question, it's a statement. And your tone suggests it's DCI Spate and his officers who are on trial here.'

'I'm seeking to discover exactly what happened at the racecourse. There is recorded evidence I could produce—' Vaughan glowered. 'This isn't a three-ring circus, or a television show. And I don't like these sarcastic comments about the police. They are good men doing a good job.'

'But not quite in the manner described by DCI Spate,' Eric contended.

Colonel Vaughan was unappeased. *Questions,* Mr Ward.' Eric turned back to DCI Spate, who was standing impassively, still gripping the rail in front of him. 'So let's move on. Why exactly did you target my client?'

Charlie Spate scowled. 'We received information.'

'That he was dealing in drugs?'

There was a brief hesitation before Spate replied. 'It was to that effect, yes.'

'And the package that was found on my client contained what you expected?'

'We didn't *expect* anything, Mr Ward. We were acting on information. It could have been wrong. As it turned out, we arrested Dieter Barschel and found him in possession of Class A prohibited—'

'So your informant was right. Is she usually reliable?' Charlie Spate opened his mouth to answer and then closed it again. After a moment he replied, 'I didn't say the informant was a woman.'

'No matter . . . but explain to me, how did you actually identify my client?'

'He was known to us.'

'To whom?'

'His records—'

'Did Detective Sergeant Adams, or any of the arresting officers, know him by sight?'

'I imagine so.'

Eric paused, raising his eyebrows in mock surprise. 'How? It's some years since my client has appeared in court, and then only for relatively minor offences. I don't believe he has any record of dealing in drugs, or links to persons who do *so*. So how could the officers, in a large crowd of people, so easily identify Dieter Barschel? Or did they find him because he was pointed out to them? DCI Spate, was he *fingered?*'

For a moment, Eric thought DCI Spate was about to explode at the insinuation. He was forestalled by the magistrate. Colonel Vaughan rapped a knuckle on the bench, impatiently. 'Mr Ward, I repeat my warnings. You're proceeding as though DCI Spate is a hostile witness and I've made no such ruling. You're implying in your questions

— or statements, it seems to me — that there has been some underhand dealing by the police, without producing any evidence to support that. Supposition is not evidence.'

'I'd be more than happy to produce the CCTV footage for inspection by the court,' Eric replied, nettled.

'And *I'd* be happy if you just went about questioning the witness properly,' Colonel Vaughan snapped. 'I keep saying, this is a preliminary hearing and you're wandering far afield, treating it as though the police are on trial here, rather than your client.'

The magistrate's voice had risen and there was a silence in the courtroom after he had finished. DCI Spate stood impassively, staring at Eric, waiting. Eric decided it was time to strike. He turned away from the bench, to face the witness. 'Do you know a man called Vasagar?'

Surprise flitted briefly across DCI Spate's features. 'I know of Mark Vasagar, yes.'

'He is a local businessman, I believe?'

'He could be described as such,' Spate replied with a hint of irony in his voice.

'And is he the owner of a night club called Nocturne?'

Charlie Spate pretended to think hard, ruminated over the question. 'I cannot be absolutely certain that he is the owner, but he is reputed to be the owner.'

'Do you ever visit that particular club?' Eric asked casually. 'I have been there in pursuit of my duties.'

Eric detected the qualification and the slight unease that underlay it. 'And what about your off-duty hours? Have you ever visited Nocturne when you were off duty?'

'When I am off duty I visit various places,' Spate replied evasively.

Eric folded his arms impassively and regarded Spate in silence for several seconds. 'Have you ever visited Nocturne for the purpose of . . . social intercourse?'

Charlie Spate didn't like the way Eric had dwelled on the last two words. He raised his chin in defiance. 'That's what clubs are for, isn't it? Social intercourse.'

Eric smiled, glanced at the magistrate, considered pressing the question and emphasising the evasiveness. Perhaps it wasn't necessary. 'When you went to Nocturne did you ever meet there a woman who went by the name of Romy Arendt?'

There was a brief silence. Spate's heart was beating furiously but he managed to affect a diffident shrug. 'In the course of my work I meet many people. In clubs and elsewhere.'

'Would you be surprised if I told you that this lady — Romy Arendt — worked occasionally as a singer at Nocturne?'

'I am never surprised by questions asked by lawyers.' Colonel Vaughan shuffled in his seat and glared at the witness. He himself was becoming impatient at the DCI's evasiveness. Charlie Spate ignored the magistrate, and waited. Eric gave a wry smile. 'I believe Romy Arendt originally came from East Germany. Would that surprise you?'

'I have no information to that effect.'

'So she isn't known to the police?' Eric asked quickly. Charlie Spate retreated somewhat; there was a wariness in his reply 'I have no information on a possible police record.'

'So you're not aware that she has twice been arrested for soliciting in the West End of Newcastle?' Eric pressed.

'I can't keep track of everything that goes on in the prostitution rackets. Or of who's involved in them.'

'Have you a good memory, DCI Spate?' Eric asked sarcastically.

Colonel Vaughan had had enough. He cleared his throat noisily and emphatically. 'Mr Ward, I keep stressing that this is a preliminary hearing, that you cannot treat DCI Spate as a hostile witness, and in any case I cannot follow any pattern, or discern any reason behind the questions you are now putting to the witness. I do not see what relevance the existence of this woman, Romy Arendt, has to the proceedings in which we are involved.'

Eric lowered his head in mock acceptance of the reproof. 'I apologise to the bench, sir. I was just getting around to asking DCI Spate what he knew of the woman's background; whether or not he was aware that the woman Romy Arendt was known to have been involved for a while in a personal relationship with my client Dieter Barschel.'

Colonel Vaughan was very still, breathing hard, his eyes fixed harshly upon Eric Ward. He was clearly in a quandary. He did not possess sufficient legal knowledge, nor experience as a magistrate, to know what to make of what was going on, or how to deal with it. His glance flickered towards the clerk of the court but he could not help. There was no matter of legal procedure involved. The magistrate was nervous and edgy; he felt that in some obscure way he was being manipulated, even mocked. He was aware there was an edge between the two men, the solicitor and the police officer, aware there was some underlying tension he was unable to identify.

He looked away from Ward, his brow creasing, to DCI Spate. Uncertainly, he said, 'You may answer the question, if you wish.'

Eric raised his eyebrows at the manner in which Colonel Vaughan had seemingly granted Spate an option in the matter. The DCI's reply was dull, flat in its tone. 'I have not been aware of a relationship between the woman Mr Ward mentions and the man we arrested for dealing in drugs.'

There was something ponderous in the statement; Spate's eyes were lidded, he seemed to be digging into his mind, seeking something out, concerns, matters that bothered him. When his glance lifted there was a deliberate blankness in his gaze. Eric Ward knew DCI Spate was lying. He felt a quick excitement; he opened his mouth to challenge the police officer but was forestalled by Colonel Vaughan.

'That's enough,' the magistrate announced decisively. 'I don't know what's going on here, but my patience is at an end. We're dealing with issues that should be dealt with elsewhere. You've made a submission of no case to answer, Mr Ward; you want me to dismiss proceedings against your client. But all I've heard so far is innuendo. You've raised issues without proof yes, all right, I'm aware you believe

41

the footage from the CCTV tapes will back up statements you've made, but even so I remain uneasy at the way you've been proceeding. I think it's time you tell the court, directly, the reasons why you believe I should dismiss these charges against your client.'

Eric took a deep breath. He was taking a chance, diving in like this into deep water. He glanced at Spate: the man's features were set, impassive. He nodded. He addressed the bench. 'All right, I will state my reasons why I believe that a miscarriage of justice is occurring here. In the first instance there are considerable holes in the prosecution case: my client has no history of drug dealing yet is targeted by three arresting officers; secondly, the account given by the arresting officers is not supported by the CCTV footage that is available; the police account is based upon the fact that, as they admit, they were proceeding on the basis of information received but they have not identified that informant. From my own enquiries I am convinced that there is a link, a matter of bad blood between my client and the woman known as Romy Arendt. There is the possibility that the instigator of these trumped-up charges against my client was actually his former lover, Romy Arendt. My client contends the drugs were planted on him. If the prosecution wishes to investigate issues such as these in more depth, in order to determine whether the woman played a significant role in the identification of Dieter Barschel, in the passing of information that he was involved in drug dealing, and how that information was passed to the police, it may be that a case can be made out. I doubt it, but that is a matter for the prosecution. I contend there is no case to answer, though there may well be a case to be raised against those who are pressing this prosecution, based upon doubtful police practices, the planting of so-called evidence, and the use of perjured testimony.'

When Eric finished and sat down there was a glazed look in Charlie Spate's eyes but his mouth has hard, his teeth bared in subdued, controlled fury. There was complete silence in the courtroom behind Eric, but there was ill-controlled anger in Colonel Vaughan's tones as he responded. 'I think this is disgraceful, Mr Ward. You have impugned the gallant police officers who have taken part in this business. The statements you have made, the challenges you have thrown out are beyond my competence to deal with. These are matters that should have been raised at a full hearing. I cannot accept that . . .' He spluttered a little, losing track of his argument in his anger at what he conceived to be an attack on the establishment he was sworn to uphold. He recovered his composure, and his tone became colder. 'I am not sure of your motives in this matter. All I can say is that there is still sufficient conviction in my mind that your client Dieter Barschel does indeed have a case to answer. It is for the prosecution to consider, in view of the remarks you have made, what steps they should follow in order to take matters further, but as far as your submission is concerned, I reject it. It is my intention to remand the accused for trial in the High Court at a date yet to be determined.'

Eric rose to his feet again. 'So now there is the earlier matter to be determined.'

'What?' Colonel Vaughan snapped. 'What are you talking about?'

'I now wish to request that bail be granted to my client on his own recognisance.'

Colonel Vaughan glared in helpless fury at Eric and then turned to the CPS solicitor. Anstruther struggled to his feet, somewhat stunned by the way things were turning out. 'I am instructed to oppose the granting of bail, sir. On the grounds already put forward.'

Eric Ward remained standing, his eyes challenging the magistrate. Colonel Vaughan hesitated; he was in a quandary. He had been angered by Eric Ward's submission and the questioning of DCI Spate but he was aware that the aspersions that had been cast upon the behaviour of the police officers could rebound upon his own conduct of the preliminary hearing, the more so if they were later proved to be true. He was inclined to find in favour of Anstruther's submission, but he hesitated: he was not long on the bench, there was the Lord Chancellor's Department view of these abnormal proceedings to consider, and the opinions of certain people in the county who had not been too supportive of his initial election to the bench. As an Army officer he had learned that strategy was all important, the future was to be regarded, and when under possible attack, defensive positions had to be strengthened. He tugged at his moustache in a nervous gesture. He glared at Eric. 'On his own recognisance, you say?'

Ten minutes later, after his application had been granted, Eric Ward made his way from the courtroom, Dieter Barschel by his side. They were besieged in the roadway outside the court by a group of reporters seeking quotations, and demanding to know what his next steps would be, what evidence he had to support his veiled accusations in the courtroom. He brushed aside the questions politely, and walked into Grey Street where he hailed a cab, bustled Dieter Barschel inside. As he made to enter the vehicle himself he felt a hand on his arm.

It was Charlie Spate.

Eric held the door open, hesitated, then stepped away from the cab. The reporters were clustered outside the steps of the magistrates' court. Only the police officer and himself stood there. There was a harshness in Spate's voice. He spoke only a few words. 'You should know, Ward. I'm not a man who forgets easily.'

He jabbed a finger in Eric's chest. 'You made a bad mistake today. A *very* bad mistake!'

CHAPTER 4

The call he had been expecting with some sullen trepidation came three days later.

It was inevitable in view of the headlines in the local newspapers. There had even been a brief flurry in the national press, with a leader in *The Times* weighing in on police corruption. Even *so*, Charlie was surprised by the speed of the reaction from the top brass. There had been a few comments of sympathy extended to him by some of the older colleagues, but on the whole the matter had been largely ignored. Elaine Start had not spoken to him about it, though she had looked at him strangely once or twice and had seemed to be on the point of asking him something. Each time she had backed off. He was grateful for that. And when the call finally came, he received it with a certain relief: he wanted to get the matter over with.

ACC Jim Charteris remained seated while Charlie stood in front of him in the ACC's office. Charteris was sitting squarely in his chair, his handsome, clean-cut features grim, and his eyes cold as he stared silently at Charlie. At last he said, menacingly, 'This has been a real balls-up, don't you agree, DCI Spate?'

Charlie raised his chin a trifle, fixed his gaze on the top of the window behind Charteris's chair and made no reply.

'If I say the Chief Constable is less than pleased it's the understatement of the century,' Charteris went on. 'When he saw the newspaper headlines he went ape. I got my arse kicked, and hard, and that's something I don't enjoy. Then we had to call a meeting with the CPS and that was more than a bit hairy, I can tell you. They were falling over themselves to dissociate themselves from blame. The Chief even insisted on seeing the CCTV footage himself. I mean, hell's flames, we're supposed to be grown men, experienced officers, and here we get the Chief saying he could do the job better himself!' He paused, eyeing Charlie suspiciously. 'I need some plain speaking from you, DCI, and I need clear, unequivocal answers. The Chief and I, we've looked at the tape closely and we've reached certain conclusions. Was that arrest of Dieter Barschel a set-up?'

'No, sir,' Charlie lied firmly. He was used to lying; he was good at it.

The stain of suspicion remained in the ACC's eyes. 'All right, that guy who gave Barschel the packet of drugs, was he known to you?'

Charlie shook his head. 'Not at the time. Since then we've done some checking and it turns out he's a small-time villain, bit of credit card fraud. He's got a record.'

'Have you pulled him in for questioning?'

'No, sir.' When the ACC seemed to be about to make an angry comment, Charlie hastened, 'I mean, we've been look-ing for him, but he seems to have gone to earth for the time being. He'll surface again: characters like him always do.'

Charteris grunted, clearly unimpressed. 'That's as may be. But why the hell wasn't he pulled in at the same time as the arrest of Barschel was made?'

Charlie licked dry lips. This was trickier to explain. He'd already gone over this with DS Adams and the other arrest-ing officers: they'd stick by the story and so would he. 'They were concentrating on the target, sir. They closed in on him and he put up a fight. It took the three of them to subdue him and—'

Charteris waved his hand in a gesture of contempt. 'Come on Spate, I've looked at the footage, and it was handbags at three paces stuff!'

'The CCTV footage might suggest that, sir, but at the time the lads thought they'd all better pile in. There was a crowd around—'

'And the character who planted the drugs was on the edge of it, noting events!'

'That's easy to say, sir, with the benefit of hindsight and the CCTV footage,' Charlie argued stubbornly. 'But at the time, the lads were doing what they had been told to do: get hold of the man with the drugs. They had a job, and they did it according to their own lights.'

'It was a bloody disaster,' Charteris snarled, leaning forward, 'and I get the feeling you're not giving me all the information you've got!'

Charlie rocked slightly on his heels but kept his eyes fixed on the window and made no reply.

Charteris sat there, staring at him. After a little while, he said, 'You've had dealings with that solicitor, Ward, before.'

Charlie scowled. 'Yes, sir. He's an ex-copper gone bad.'

'The Press think he's a shining bloody light!' Charteris countered. 'We're the ones who are coming out of this with mud on our faces!' He paused. 'Where did Ward get his information?'

'I don't know; sir. And what he came up with, it's just guesswork, supposition, mud-slinging, rather than hard information.'

'Is that so?' sneered Charteris. 'From all accounts he asked some pertinent, and rather damaging questions.'

'It was innuendo, sir, not based on facts—'

'Spate, I'll ask you one more time,' Charteris interrupted coldly. 'Was that a set-up?'

'No, sir.' Sweat began to trickle at the back of Charlie's neck.

'It was an arrest based on information received.'

'Yes, sir.'

'By you?'

Charlie hesitated, squared his shoulders, made no reply. Charteris leaned forward again, elbows on his desk. His tone was edged with menace. 'It was information received by you and passed on to the arresting officers. I want the name of your informant.'

Charlie grimaced. 'I'd rather you didn't ask me that, sir.'

'I'm asking you,' Charteris insisted.

'It could compromise other enquiries, sir. I've promised my informant anonymity: the source is good and has been helpful in the past. I wouldn't want to lose—'

'We're on the same side, Spate! If you can't trust a fellow officer . . . and a senior one at that . . .' Charteris's voice died away and he regarded Charlie speculatively for what seemed an age. At last he murmured, 'All right. Perhaps it's best I don't know . . . at this stage. But let's make this very clear to you, DCI. This is something that's on your plate, and it's something you've got to get sorted. It's your arse that's in the sling here, not mine, not the Chief's. And if it doesn't get sorted, well, let me put it like this . . . for you, it's what they call last chance saloon. As I recall, you didn't arrive here from the Met with the cleanest of reputations. All right, your work here has been commended — though not by me — and you've had another leg up the promotional ladder. But that doesn't mean you're fireproof. Watch your step, Charlie Spate. And I want to hear nothing more about this operation. If anything else emerges of a damaging nature, injurious to the reputation of the force, you'll be out on your neck, permanently.' He paused, then added sourly, 'And I'll tell you this. If it was for me to decide, you'd be booted out now: The Chief thinks it's better to let things hang loose, wait for the noise to fade. He thinks giving you the push could cause more trouble than keeping you, because of the consequent publicity. So you're still in harness. But don't let it choke you.'

For the first time in days Charlie felt a flood of relief flow through his veins. He lowered his gaze, met the ACC's cold glance. 'So where does that leave the case against Barschel, sir?'

'We've had discussions with the CPS. It won't be proceeded with.'

Charlie was annoyed. 'But—'

'That damned solicitor Ward got him out on bail,' Charteris snapped. 'Normally, that's no big deal, but with the stuff Ward started throwing about in the courtroom we can't afford to proceed! You're telling me there's nothing to it, but I'm taking no chances and the Chief agrees. If any of that stuff is true it could come out at the full hearing and you can just guess what play some smart-arse barrister would make of that. The Chief doesn't want to take the chance. So the whole business will end quietly, with a warning to Barschel — and to you.'

'Dropping the case, it'll look bad, sir.'

'And continuing with it could explode in our faces. In any case, carrying on could compromise other, more serious operations.'

That was it. Now it was coming out, Charlie thought. He was being made a scapegoat, so their backs were covered while they were after some other game. Anger seethed in his veins. 'Will that be all, sir?'

Charteris glared at him. 'That will be all, DCI Spate, but remember what I said. Keep your head down and your nose clean — and steer clear of your precious informant. The Dieter Barschel case is closed, keep away from him, leave it all alone. Now get the hell out of here!'

The fury was still a red hot iron in his chest when Charlie went down to the canteen. He got himself a coffee and sat there for a while, alone. A few other officers came in, glanced his way but sat elsewhere. He was happy about that. He'd been thinking hard for the last few days, working out just what he should do. He had serious scores to settle, that was for sure, but he had to go about it carefully. It wasn't so much now that Dieter Barschel had been set up — it was the fact that DCI Charlie Spate had been made a fool of by his informant. He took out his mobile phone and flicked up the call list. He stared at one particular number for a little while, considering, then slowly proceeded to delete it. A mobile wasn't a safe piece of equipment if you wanted to hide something.

He finished his coffee, then left the building. He drove into town, parked in a quiet back road in Jesmond and found a telephone booth. It was in the state he would have expected: starred windows where a bottle had been smashed against the toughened glass, obscene graffiti scrawled on the paintwork, a few telephone numbers and a scattering of cards offering personal massages on the floor. He picked up the receiver. It was still in use. He pressed the call buttons, punching out the numbers he had memorised from his mobile call list. The phone rang for a long while at the other end. He was on the point of replacing the receiver when there was a click and a voice came on the line. It was a man.

'Hello?'

Charlie made no reply.

'Hello? Who's there?' There was a short pause, a muttered curse, and then the phone was slammed down.

Charlie grimaced, put down the receiver and went back to his car. He sat in the driving seat for a few minutes, thinking, working out the possibilities. A man's voice. It couldn't be a client. And Charlie knew of no regular. And no pimp either, for that matter. He started the engine, drove slowly out of the back street and headed for the address he had always visited after dark.

There was a white van parked outside the apartment. As Charlie drove past slowly he saw a tall, Asian man leave the van carrying some heavy boxes into the hallway. He looked up to the windows of the apartment: new curtains. His guess was there'd be a new tenant at the flat. It made sense, if he thought about it. She'd have had to do a runner, now that things had blown up the way they had. Maybe that had always been her intention anyway. He gritted his teeth: rabbits could run but there was always a way of ferreting them out of a burrow. He'd be patient: there was time. He was off the hook for the moment, but he'd get his revenge in due course.

Against her. And against that bastard Eric Ward.

* * *

For Eric Ward himself there had been considerable irritation during the days after the Dieter Barschel hearing. Barschel himself had wanted to get away to avoid the hounding from reporters that was inevitable. He had asked Eric for help; finally Eric had rung his ex-wife, Anne, and explained things to her. She'd come up with a good suggestion. Though the Sedleigh Hall estates were largely grouped near the Cheviots there were a few properties scattered elsewhere. One was to the south-east, in County Durham: an isolated cottage in Weardale.

'I'm grateful,' he had said sincerely to his ex-wife.

'If you've got a problem, why shouldn't you turn to me?' Anne had asked, laughing.

Their relationship had recently achieved a more balanced level: the trauma she had gone through when her lover Jason Sullivan had got involved in fraudulent activity seemed to have abated. Eric had visited her regularly during that period, helped her through the problems; they had taken long walks together in the hills, bringing back memories of happier days, and many of the difficulties of the past seemed to have disappeared. Much of the old bitterness had faded, each had come to terms with their separation and they had achieved an amicable agreement: there were some things that did not get talked about, for there was no point in raking over cold ashes of resentment.

But while Dieter Barschel had managed to escape the attentions of the reporters, Eric had not. It was not exactly a hounding by the Press, but it certainly had considerable nuisance value. He had been in the business for some years now; but his practice was not exactly of the flashy kind: the big firms in the city tended to get the cases which drew public attention. Eric's clients were generally small people, shady individuals who operated along the waterfront, often just on the right side of the law. They drew little attention beyond the odd paragraph in the local newspaper, so by and large Eric was rarely in the public eye. There had from time to time been bigger issues to deal with of course, in the past: when he had been retained by his ex-wife's company there had been times when he had dealt with major corporate transactions. But it was not a field that he found satisfying: the chicanery to be found in corporate boardrooms had irritated him. Somehow he felt better about himself when dealing with little people: there was a greater sense of reality about their lives. It had been one of the causes of friction between himself and Anne.

But now he found himself being door-stepped by reporters as he left his office, usually wanting to try to dredge more from him than he had revealed in court. And there had been questions about his tactics. He was aware there had been some mutterings in the Law Society; a brief, critical reference to it in the *Law Gazette*. His performance at the preliminary hearing had also caused him a certain amount of self-searching. It had been a risky procedure. The work Jackie Parton had done, rooting out possible relationships, pointing out curious behaviour on the CCTV footage, retailing the whispers that were going around the pubs and clubs along the Tyne, had been something he had used, and relied upon, but it had been a dangerous tactic before Colonel Vaughan: many of the accusations he had made, or implied, had yet to be proved. He had talked it over with Jackie Parton, a few days after the preliminary hearing. They had met in a West End pub, the Hydraulic Engine, and sat in the back room.

'If we'd gone to trial with only what you'd given me, we could have been in trouble,' Eric had suggested. 'At a full hearing I think some of it could have been thrown out of court. Unless we could back it up with concrete proof. And one or two reporters have twigged that. They've hinted that maybe I was flying kites I couldn't control.'

Jackie Parton had shrugged. 'Aye, well, all I can say is that I think the footage shows the truth. The polis had set it up: there was a plant and they knew it was going to happen. I've done a check, by the way: I've found out the guy who slipped the package on Barschel is called Bennie Archer and it looks as though he got slipped a wad for doing it. Not by the polis, though, that's the odd thing. No chatter that they paid him. Besides, he's not around the river any more — so he obviously got enough to scarper. Or,' Jackie added reflectively, 'maybe he's scared.'

'Of what?' Eric had asked curiously.

'Well, the picture's a bit blurred like,' Jackie remarked thoughtfully. 'I mean, you look at it one way and it seems clear enough: the polis get a tip-off, they react to it even if it's only a small collar — I mean, it helps the statistics in the war against drug dealing, don't it? The fact Barschel is only a small fish don't matter. The fact he's not really involved in the drug scene, that don't matter either. But then, when you look at it another way . . . why was Barschel set up anyway? Who was grinding an axe in this? Who really gave the polis the information?'

'The woman in the case, it would seem. The one you named as Romy Arendt.'

Jackie grimaced. 'Well, there you go again. Mebbe it was so. But what was in it for her?'

'Surely, once you found that she was linked to Barschel, a couple of years back, it could always have been just a matter of a woman scorned, getting her revenge on an ex-lover. I mean, that's the supposition I was working on.'

Jackie Parton shook his head doubtfully and sipped at the pint glass in his hand. 'That's what I was thinking at the time, but since, well, I keep wonderin'. I mean, Romy is a hooker; she's on the game for money. Why would she get so involved? OK, so she got her claws into a copper and no doubt gave him a free ride, so to speak. But I mean, using a contact she'd made with the polis . . . it was takin' a big chance, queering her own pitch, so to speak.' He glanced at

Eric ruminatively. 'And she's gone on the hop too, I'm told. She ain't been seen in Nocturne for more than a while. Still, it may be a mystery we'll never solve.'

'The workings of a woman's mind?' Eric asked, smiling. 'That, and just exactly what all this was about.'

'But you've firmed up on the connection between this Romy Arendt and DCI Spate?' Eric queried thoughtfully.

Jackie Parton wriggled his wiry frame in doubt. 'I can't be absolutely certain, Mr Ward. There's been talk. She worked at Nocturne, and she had an apartment in Jesmond. There's a whisper among some of the girls that Charlie Spate had been getting some around there, but you know how it is, often just chatter and if we had had to get some firm evidence . . . well, these girls have to earn a living and they'd be reluctant to talk.'

'Do you think Romy Arendt herself would talk?'

'You'd have to find her first, Mr Ward.' The ex-jockey shook his head doubtfully. 'It's like I say; When I first came to you with the chatter, and the connections, and the possibilities . . . well, it was up to you how you used it all, and I thought I'd be able to get more on it all after a while. But that's not the way it is. That nark Bennie Archer has skipped, and so has Romy Arendt. Probably down to the Smoke. But runnin' away, and settin' up elsewhere, it takes funds . . . and like I said, maybe fear, to do that. But what's the edge in it? Why is it that no one's saying anything more about it now?'

Eric sighed. 'At least Barschel's off the hook. I've heard, unofficially, that the charges against him will not be proceeded with. They'll lie on the file, of course, but it's likely we'll hear no more.'

'He'll be happy about that,' Jackie asserted confidently. Eric was not so certain: happiness was hardly the right word to describe Barschel's frame of mind.

CHAPTER 5

Dieter Barschel had been in a strange mood when Eric had taken him out to the farm cottage deep in the hills of Weardale. Eric had tried to talk gently to him, make him relax somewhat after the tension of the recent days. They were travelling on the south side of the river and Eric pointed out the nature of the hill farming country, the cultivated 'intake' fields from the surrounding heather-strewn moorlands, explaining how the pattern of the land and the farming year were shaped arid dictated by the breeding habits of sheep. It was a narrow dale they passed through with roads, old railway and river in close proximity to one another and they drove past roadside verges crowded with fronds of sweet cicely. 'It gives off a strong fragrance of aniseed when the leaves are crushed,' Eric explained. 'It's sometimes used by the wives of local farmers as a sweetener for jams.'

Dieter Barschel had been unimpressed, and indeed was clearly barely listening. Sweet cicely jostling for roadside space with meadow cranesbill was an irrelevance for him. His heavy brow was furrowed, his eyes narrowed and Eric detected a feeling of intense, suppressed fury, seething in the man, close to explosive release.

They were in old railway country where the steam engines had run up steep gradients and through deep tunnels to haul trucks of lime, ironstone and lead ore in the old days. Now it was a land of high bare fells, snow-laced in winter, north-facing gullies and a farming area where haymaking could be as late as July or August.

When they reached the somewhat dilapidated farm cottage they unloaded Barschel's gear. He had brought little: a backpack and a suitcase. When Eric hefted it, he was surprised at its weight. Barschel took it from him immediately.

'It's just some papers and books,' he grunted.

Barschel had then made a quick inspection of the two-bedroomed, sparsely furnished stone cottage and expressed a brief satisfaction. He looked out at the single stone track that wound up from the dale below to the cottage, and asked what the cottage had been used for previously.

'In the winter,' Eric explained, 'the shepherds would use it if they were stranded. Before that, a century ago, it would have been the home of lead miners. My ex-wife and I, we used it occasionally, when we walked in the hills about here. Usually when I had business in County Durham.'

'And I am secure here?'

Eric was curious, noting the nervous edge to the man's tone. 'Certainly. But from what? I don't understand why you need to hide away. The police have been embarrassed — they won't be bothering you, while they work out what to do about the charges against you. And as for reporters, well, the noise is dying down now.'

'It is not the police I fear, or the reporters,' Barschel muttered bitterly. 'And what about the woman?'

'Romy Arendt?' Eric hesitated. 'What exactly happened between the two of you?'

Barschel had been reluctant to talk about her. When Jackie Parton had discovered the relationship, Eric had asked Barschel about it but he had been reticent. He had agreed finally to the tactics which Eric had used in the preliminary hearing but it was with a certain lack of interest: he seemed to be preoccupied with other matters. There was a dissonance between his concern that a case was being brought against him — which he still insisted was a set-up — and the fury that seemed to be building inside him. Even the part played by the woman seemed somehow an irrelevance. But here at the farm cottage he was briefly prepared to say more.

'I lived with her for a year or so,' he muttered, passing a hand over his brow in a gesture of annoyance. 'It was a matter of convenience, and little more. She came from East Germany, you know; and I'd lived there for a while. She needed a place to stay; it was some years since I had been with a woman, other than for what you English call the one-night stand. It was . . . good enough.' He scowled as he stared out of the window; 'Then we quarrelled. She had become established in her work; there was the nightclub. There were other men, and better clothes. We had a disagreement. So I threw her out. It was . . . there was violence.'

He flashed a quick, angry glance towards Eric: there was a bruising of suspicion in his eyes, a hard determination in the set of his mouth. 'But the woman is a distraction, an irrelevance. All this, it is not about her. You must understand, it has been as I said to you at the beginning. I have never been involved in drugs. This was done by the police. But it is not them, it is not the police who are behind this attempt to silence me. I have knowledge, there are things I could say and now I am angry. There are some things I must do, some telephone calls—'

'There's no line here,' Eric said, uncomfortable at the man's vehemence.

'I have my mobile phone. It will suffice.'

'I'm not sure you're wise in pursuing what you're hinting at,' Eric remarked cautiously. 'If you think you know why you were set up, talk to me, maybe we can get some recompense, some compensation—'

Barschel had stared at him, almost uncomprehendingly. 'Recompense? That is an easy word! No, I have been subjected to this attack for one reason only. I intend to react to it. Then, when this is all over and I have achieved what I set out to do, perhaps we will talk again. I will explain things to you. And believe me, there will be interesting things to hear.'

His tone was intense, his brow furrowed, a clear, angry determination in his features.

Eric frowned. 'I still think you should confide in me now. There are things I could do to assist—'

'No.' The voice was sharp. 'Where I come from, matters such as these are dealt with on a personal level. Meanwhile, if I can stay here, and you will tell no one of my location—'

'You're safe here,' Eric promised. 'And we should know in a week or so just what the prosecution finally decides to do. We've taken a risk but . . .'

It was a gamble that had paid off. His secretary Susie had a contact in the courts administration who, Eric teased from time to time, would answer her queries because he was clearly sweet on her; she had had a quiet conversation with him and she had then passed on the hint to Eric. The police would not be taking the matter further. It would be quietly filed away.

But the newspaper reporters had no inkling of that and during the next ten days they continued to keep tabs on Eric as he got on with his work at the Quayside. They were there at the court on the Tuesday morning, in some force, but it was probably because of the combination — Eric Ward, the solicitor who had challenged the police force he had worked with years earlier, and a hearing that involved a three-foot snake that had appeared in the cylinder cupboard of a terraced house in Benton.

The plaintiff housewife was short, plump and indignant. She was seeking an injunction, and also damages for nervous shock and the enforced need to uproot herself to live with a sister she disliked.

'Just how did you come upon the snake, Mrs Charlton?' Eric asked gently.

'Well, I use the cylinder cupboard, where the hot water tank is, to dry the clothes because it's warm in there. And there it was, this 'orrible long thing, and I screamed and I run downstairs.' She hitched her forearms under her ample bosom in displeasure. 'The fact is, that Mr Donald, he kept them in his house next door: there was more than twenty-four snakes in there, and he kept tarantulas and other creepy things as well! I got onto the council and Mr Donald eventually admitted he was causing a nuisance but said he was doing nothing wrong legally . . .'

The solicitor acting for Mr Donald had pointed out to the court that the animals kept were not listed in the Schedule to the Dangerous Wild Animals Act 1976, and his client had since improved security to a considerable extent. Eric had engaged an expert who confirmed that even in the best regulated circumstances snakes tended to escape.

'They're like moggies,' Mrs Charlton affirmed.

'Cats?' Eric asked, mystified as a ripple of laughter surged around the courtroom.

'Aye, you know. Cats are always wanderin'. So's snakes. Anyway, I been under the doctor, and he's told me I'm sufferin' from a new . . . new . . .'

'Neurosis?' Eric suggested.

'That's it. It's why I had to go and live with me sister, and we don't get on and it's not right havin' to move just because Mr Donald wants to keep wild animals like snakes and monity . . . monity . . .'

'Monitor lizards,' Eric supplied.

He had managed to obtain an injunction against Mr Donald to cease keeping his pets, with damages to be assessed for nervous shock and the inconvenience of removal from the family home. There were some broad smiles among the jostling of local reporters as he made his way out of the county court. Most of them he recognised: the local newspapers tended to send the same young people to cover the local issues. But the woman who stopped him at the top of the steps was unknown to him.

'Mr Ward . . . May I have a word?'

She was perhaps thirty years of age but looked younger; her manner was assured, confident, but she had the open, innocent face of a teenager. Her eyes were wide-spaced, her irises green. She had fair hair, simply dressed, long in the back with a fringe that half concealed the shapely arch of her eyebrows. She was dressed in a loose sweater that hid her figure but left enough hints of her shapeliness. Her mouth was wide, her lower lip full and sensual. Her nose and cheeks were lightly freckled: she had, he felt, a Nordic look about her.

'I'm sorry, I'm just on the way back to my office.'

She stood in front of him, determinedly. 'It's about Dieter Barschel.'

He sighed. 'I hoped for a moment it was about monitor lizards and snakes.'

'I'm sorry?'

Perhaps she had not been in the courtroom. He shook his head, slightly exasperated. 'I take it you are a reporter.'

For a moment he thought she hesitated, as though prepared to deny it. Then she nodded.

Eric shook his head. 'Well, let me say there's no further activity on the Dieter Barschel front. While I've yet to receive official confirmation that the charges against him will not be proceeded with, I can say that as far as I'm concerned it's highly likely that my representation of Mr Barschel will shortly come to an end — he'll not need my further services. So I hardly think you'd find a conversation with me rewarding.' He glanced behind him somewhat ruefully at other, departing journalists. 'My involvement with Mr Barschel has been somewhat . . . well, it's caused some excitement, of the kind I'm happy to do without. But in essence, I think it's probably over. So, if you'll excuse me- '

'I've come from Berlin.'

Eric stared at her. He noted a certain pugnacity about her jaw, a determination in her green eyes. 'You can't be suggesting that German newspapers have been interested in this business?' he asked wonderingly.

'I arrived here late last week. In London I saw an account of this case against Barschel. So I came north. I wish to speak with him.'

Eric hesitated, puzzled. 'You want to talk with him about this drugs charge?'

She gave an irritated, dismissive shake of her head. 'I want to interview him on other matters. Nothing to do with drugs. I want to talk with him about the old days.'

She stood squarely in front of him, chin up, holding his glance.

He remembered Dieter Barschel's angry, insistent determination to pursue his own course. The woman, her interest in Barschel intrigued him. 'Perhaps you'd better come along with me to my office . . .'

* * *

Susie Cartwright brought in the coffee and behind the young woman's back rolled her eyes at her employer. She clearly felt his client list was improving in pulchritude if not in earnings possibilities. Eric waited until she had closed the door behind her before addressing the young woman facing him across his desk. 'I think we should begin by introductions. You'll know my name is Ward, otherwise you wouldn't have approached.'

'You are a lawyer, representing Dieter Barschel.'

He nodded. 'I was representing him. Now; I'm not so sure. It's likely our relationship is ending. And you are . . . ?'

She frowned slightly. 'A reporter, as I said. Freelance. With a German magazine of some reputation. My name . . . it is Hannah Witt.'

He smiled. 'I congratulate you on your English. And your accent.'

'I went to a finishing school in Switzerland. We had English teachers.'

'And you have an interest in Dieter Barschel. May I ask what that interest may be? You've already said it has nothing to do with the charges of drug dealing that he's recently faced.'

There was a short silence. She looked at her hands, then shrugged. 'It is simply explained. I wish to interview him, for an article that I am preparing for the magazine. He was a well-known footballer at one time, you know; in Germany as well as Italy and Spain.'

She was being evasive. 'That was twenty years ago,' Eric reminded her gently, 'and he was never that famous. Who would be interested in reading about him now?'

She stared at him. 'It is not simply the football I want to talk to him about. There is his background. Where he grew up.'

'In Romania?'

There was something odd about her, something unprofessional for a reporter. She seemed ill at ease. Possibly there were things she did not want to talk about, but that was none of his business. And his representation of Dieter Barschel was virtually ended. 'I need to explain,' Eric said gently, 'that if you're not interested in what's been happening here in Newcastle there's little I can do to help you. Mr Barschel has never talked to me about his earlier life, and even if he had I wouldn't be able to disclose it because of client confidentiality. So, I'm not sure—'

'You know where he is living,' she interrupted him.

He was prepared neither to deny nor confirm the fact. She read it in his eyes.

'It is important that I talk with him,' she said. Suddenly there was a pleading note in her voice.

Eric hesitated. 'I'm not sure that I can help you. Mr Barschel specifically asked me to ensure he was not bothered by reporters or others while he awaits a decision from the Crown Prosecution Service. I don't feel—'

Her words came out in a desperate rush, as though she was terrified he was going to dismiss her. 'Did you know that in 1982 a businessman by the name of Karl Harms, who had been jailed for life for spying for the American Central Intelligence Agency, was found suffocated in his cell in the East German prison Bautzen?' Her lips were pale. 'It was on the first day in April.'

Eric's eyes widened. 'I don't see what this has to do with—'

'The official account stated categorically that Harms had committed suicide. But some doubt must be cast on that verdict.'

'Why?' Eric was intrigued, in spite of himself.

'He was due to be taken to the West in a spy swap arrangement, just a few weeks later. If you were on the point of gaining your freedom in such circumstances would you decide to end your life?'

Eric picked up his coffee cup, took a sip, set it down and stared at it for a little while. 'What does this have to do with Dieter Barschel?' he asked.

'That is what I wish to determine,' she replied.

Eric stared at his coffee cup, indeterminate. 'I'm afraid,' he said after a short pause, 'you'll have to give me a bit more than that before I can go against my client's wishes.'

Hannah Witt looked past him, towards the window. Her eyes were suddenly blank, as though she had turned her gaze inwards to decide what to say next, seeking the right words. Eric waited.

'If I tell you that there is a strong possibility that the death of Karl Harms is likely to be linked to the disappearance of the head of a construction firm based in Hamburg will that be enough? Particularly when the man in question was working for one of a network of companies secretly owned by the SED, the Socialist Unity Party. He was known to have entered into conversations with various functionaries of the German Democratic Republic.'

Eric gave a sigh of frustration. 'I don't understand . . . I still don't see that I can be of assistance to you. None of this has relevance to Dieter Barschel, as far as I am aware.'

Her gaze turned to him. The green eyes were intense. 'A month ago a headless corpse in a plastic bag was fished out of the Rhine. It is said that the body was that of the man I mention, the head of the Hamburg construction firm.'

Eric spread his hands wide. 'Miss Witt—'

'According to employment records that I have copies of, Dieter Barschel worked in that firm in some undefined capacity before he left for Italy. You should understand, Mr Ward, these two deaths I mention, they are not unique. There appear to have been at least twelve people who have been similarly eliminated. All had such connections. I want to talk to Dieter Barschel, because I strongly believe that his life also is in danger. Is that reason enough, Mr Ward?'

It was.

* * *

The afternoon was darkening as they drove past the stone-built lime kilns that had been used years earlier for the burning of limestone to produce agricultural and industrial lime. For a while they were in a decayed world of mounds and water against a screened background of tall cliff edges. The sun was low in the sky, setting red in the west and scarring the brown, thin soil of the spoil heaps with a golden edge, glinting in the oases that lay between the rock and the sandy earth. Eric was silent as they drove, pondering over what Hannah Witt had said, and concerned that he might be doing the wrong thing. He was taking her on trust with her innocent face and eager intensity: she seemed to want to warn Barschel about something, as well as obtain other information from him. But she had refused to disclose more. He had the feeling that just as he doubted her, she did not really trust him. Perhaps she had had bad experiences with lawyers. Many people had.

They topped the rise and the dale spread out before their eyes. There were walkers about: a car with tinted windows was parked a little way off the road, under the shadow of the craggy rock. It was good walking country, though few seemed to use its heights. It was why he and Anne had enjoyed coming here for its loneliness and isolation.

They drove down the narrow winding road past stone walls and unkempt hedges, crossing ancient pack bridges over the hurrying stream that ate away at the millstone grit and skirting deserted stone quarries, forlorn cliffs above damp stony floors.

'The cottage is about a half mile away now. We'll be there soon.'

There was no smoke from the single chimney. The cottage had a deserted air, but that was to be expected: it was some years since he and Anne had furnished it as a base for some of their walks — it was an inconvenient distance from the main holdings of her property company, based at Sedleigh Hall. But if Dieter Barschel was not inside, he would not be far away: Eric had driven him here, and Barschel had no car. The nearest village was eight miles distant. They had made the arrangement that when Barschel wanted to leave the cottage he would phone Eric at his office.

Eric sounded his horn as he parked the car in the small yard beside the stone house. He noted that there was some repair work necessary on the end gable: ivy had crawled up the stone work, making its destructive way up towards the roof. They left the car and Eric called out. There was no reply. The front door of the cottage was ajar: Eric hesitated. Perhaps Barschel was out walking in the dale. He stepped inside, Hannah Witt just behind him. The sitting room to the right was empty: similarly the small room on the left. With one hand on the balustrade Eric looked upstairs, called out Barschel's name, wondering if he was resting in one of the two bedrooms. There was no answer. He became aware of the persistent buzzing of flies.

They found him in the kitchen at the back.

At least, Eric assumed it was Dieter Barschel. Hannah Witt made a small whimpering sound when she saw the discarded shotgun lying to one side on the stone-flagged floor. Eric stepped in front of her to shield her from the horror of the sight in the corner of the room. Most of the man's face had been shattered by the explosion from the shotgun barrel. Blood stained the front of the open-necked shirt. The body lay on its back, flung carelessly down by the force of the firepower. The arms were flung wide, loose, the fingers lightly clenched. The man would have died quickly.

Eric could only guess at the identity but it was a fair assumption to make, now, that Hannah Witt would not be getting her desired interview with ex-footballer Dieter Barschel.

CHAPTER 6

Charlie Spate was still burning.

He had done as he had been ordered by Charteris and kept a low profile, but he was still smarting and determined to find out why he had been made a fool of, and who was behind it. He visited the nightclubs several times, and kept an eye open on the late departures from Nocturne. He was bleary-eyed at work but colleagues seemed to avoid him as though he was suffering from some infectious disease. Maybe they were wary of his short temper; maybe they feared guilt by association. The ACC's warning was common knowledge at the station. And they noted his puffy-cheeked appearance after the late nights he was keeping.

Elaine Start also kept her distance. She had been given her assignment by Charteris and Charlie knew she'd be working on it with her usual assiduity. But she barely spoke to him. If he were to raise it with her he guessed that her answer would be pressure of work. And at the back of his eyelids he still had visions of the recent past: the warmth of the bed in the apartment, the woman's body against his, the treacherous whispering in his ear.

He finally decided he had to bite the bullet.

Mark Vasagar owned an apartment in Gosforth, but his main residence was on a private estate a few miles outside Newcastle. The houses were modern, well screened by security cameras, with a guard on the gateway that led along sweeping drives towards a discreetly hidden group of manicured lawns fronting elegant, mock-classical houses. Each had its Doric columns, its pretentious entrance, its mullioned windows and servants' quarters. It was known among the police as Hernando's Hideaway, after the Spanish-American financier who was said to have invested ill-gotten gains in the building of the estate, reputedly as a way of laundering cash from drugs and prostitution operations in France. As usual, nothing could be proved, in spite of Interpol files on the financier. More certainly, there was a view that while it was home to an affluent group of prominent businessmen and overpaid sportsmen, it also gave sanctuary to a number of villains who were not afraid to flaunt their wealth. Charlie thought the whole complex was tasteless and vulgar in design, but guessed he'd live there too, if he could afford it. As if.

He flashed his ID to the gateman and as he drove in he glanced in his rear mirror: the gateman was on the phone. Vasagar would now be expecting him. As he parked the car in front of Vasagar's house the ornate front door was already open: the man loosely described as a butler was standing on the front steps. He was big, athletically built with a scarred face and the bulging biceps of a weightlifter: among men in Vasagar's lines of business that was the usual model. Charlie ignored him as he ran up the steps and entered the house: the man eyed him impassively, followed him in and closed the door behind him.

'The games room, at the back and to the right,' the butler intoned gruffly.

Charlie followed the directions.

Mark Vasagar was practising, leaning over the snooker table with a cue in his hands. He was dressed in dark slacks and a white, open-necked shirt. His feet were bare. He was a tall, slim man, with dark eyes and dark skin. As far as Charlie knew, he had been born in Sri Lanka of mixed Portuguese and Indian descent: Charlie had heard that there were a considerable number of businessmen of such ancestry in Kandy, but the whisper was that Vasagar had started his successful rise to fortune in Malacca, in peninsular Malaysia. Charlie doubted that it was merely the climate that had persuaded Vasagar to leave and come to England. He would have recognised the better prospects he had in England, with continuing contacts in south-east Asia. What was certain, he had quickly built up a business empire in the north-east, an empire of some consequence that Charlie, and others, suspected had been acquired — and paid for — by Vasagar from Mad Jack Tenby, the former crime baron along the river. Now retired, by all accounts, and enjoying a social life of quality. Nothing had yet been pinned on Vasagar, but if Charlie had his way it would be only a matter of time.

The room was long, richly carpeted, and the pool table glowed greenly under the overhead light. It shone on Vasagar's smooth, luxuriant black hair. He was taking a long pot on the blue: it vanished into the pocket with a solid, satisfying clunk. Vasagar stood upright: his smile was brilliant, his attitude relaxed. 'DCI Spate. You're welcome, as always. It's a little early, but would you care for a drink?'

Charlie wasn't so stupid as to turn down the offer, however much he might be seething. Vasagar always had the best. 'Whisky. Straight.'

'*Comme d'habitude,*' Vasagar said, smiling softly as he laid down his cue and walked towards a semicircular bar built against the far wall.

Charlie grunted. He was always suspiciously resentful about men who spoke several languages. He watched as Vasagar selected a bottle of expensive malt whisky, and poured Charlie a generous glass. Vasagar took mineral water himself: a careful man, abstemious in his habits. He waved towards a plushly padded bench near the window, which looked out upon a finely mown lawn. Both men sat down. Vasagar sipped his drink. 'You play snooker, Mr Spate?'

Charlie thought of the smoky, evil-smelling billiards halls of his youth. He shook his head. 'I had a deprived childhood.' Charlie tasted the drink handed to him. It was good.

'I came late to the game,' Vasagar admitted. 'Invented in India, you know, by bored officers of the Raj. But I am told that, fortunately, I have a certain capacity for most games. Tennis, squash, billiards and snooker . . . but not, of course, the violent games enjoyed by the masses.'

Charlie nodded. Vasagar would leave the violence to others: he would pull strings, employ hard-faced men with muscle to use their fists, feet and any implements that were necessary. That was the difference between Vasagar and his predecessor Mad Jack Tenby. Mad Jack had often used a pick handle himself: Vasagar was too sophisticated to do that. He'd get his way in more subtle fashion. That was why he'd always be more difficult to pin down: slippery as a snake.

Vasagar's dark eyes were touched with a slight amusement as he sipped his drink and watched Charlie, as though guessing his thought processes. 'This visit is somewhat unexpected, but maybe I should have guessed you might pay a call on me.'

'Why?'

Vasagar shrugged carelessly. 'In view of your recent . . . problems.'

Charlie's mouth was dry with suppressed anger. 'You'd know all about my problems, of course.'

'There is talk,' Vasagar replied airily. 'So where is she?'

Vasagar's dark eyes widened in innocent incomprehension. 'She? Who are you talking about? I am not celibate, but there are no women here. The occasional overnight stay, I admit—'

'You know who I'm talking about.'

'*Whom* . . .' Vasagar corrected, gently. Charlie glared. He knew Vasagar was mocking him as the Sri Lankan pretended to think hard, considering, furrowing his brow. 'I did follow the newspaper reports of your recent . . . experience in the courtroom. The charges against that former football player, the Romanian, Barschel. Ah, yes, there was mention by the defence solicitor of a woman . . . what was her name . . . ?'

'Romy Arendt,' Charlie ground out harshly.

Vasagar swirled the mineral water in his glass, and nodded, approving of its sparkle. 'I remember now. That's right. Romy Arendt.'

'So where is she?' Charlie demanded.

Vasagar permitted himself a slight smile. 'I haven't the faintest idea.'

'You employed her.'

'Did I? In what capacity?' Vasagar's dark eyebrows were raised innocently.

'She worked at your nightclub, Nocturne.'

Vasagar affected a puzzled air. 'I don't understand, Mr Spate. First of all, Nocturne cannot really be described as my property. It is, I believe, owned by a consortium of businessmen, by way of a limited company of which I am not even a director. It's possible I do have some shares in that company. And as for working for me . . . the way I do business, you should understand, is that I make certain managerial appointments, and I leave it to others to employ people who do not fall into that senior category. Of course, I'm happy to take your word that this young woman worked at Nocturne but I can't say that I ever met her. As to knowing of her whereabouts . . . so she has disappeared, this Romy Arendt?'

Levels of responsibility, a chain of command. But Charlie wasn't fooled by Vasagar's response. The Sri Lankan would always keep his own finger on the pulse of his operations, even if he didn't get personally involved in such matters.

'If I get hold of her, maybe I'll get the answers I want,' Charlie snarled. 'But I thought it might be easier, finding out from you.'

'Finding out what, may I ask?'

Charlie sipped the whisky; suddenly the taste was sour in his throat. 'I want to know why I was set up. I want to know why I was used by you and her.'

'I don't understand, Mr Spate. I have no animus towards you.'

Animus. Charlie had plenty of animus for them both. He hated Vasagar's guts, and one of these days he'd bring the smooth bastard down. 'I know it was you, Vasagar. She worked for you. She got her instructions from one of your minions. She followed orders, set me up, so that I'd arrange to target Dieter Barschel. If I found her, maybe I'd get the truth out of her. But it's always better, I suppose, to go to the top. Just *why* did you want Barschel targeted? What's this all about? Was he muscling into your drugs set-up? What's your interest in Dieter Barschel? How has he been stepping out of line?'

Vasagar watched him carefully for a few seconds, then laid down his glass with an elaborate care. Barefooted on the plush carpet he padded back to the snooker table, picked up his cue, eyed the scattering of balls on the table. 'You're wasting your time, Mr Spate. I know nothing of this business.'

'Bullshit!'

Vasagar glanced quickly at him for a moment, as though offended. But there was something else there in his glance, a veiled uncertainty. 'Your language is colourful, Mr Spate, but as unimpressive as your grasp of reality. You are talking to the wrong man about this affair. Of course, if we were to become . . . *friends,* it is possible I would be able to help you, talk to a few people—'

Charlie was enraged. He glared at Vasagar, despising his arrogance, his wealth, his elegant, smooth appearance. 'The day I need your assistance, become what you call a friend . . .' He began to splutter in his fury. *'Friend . . .* I'd rather rot in hell. Which is where I intend putting you over this business. I'm going to get you, Vasagar. For one hell of a lot of reasons!'

Vasagar leaned over the table, eyeing the shot. But when he attempted it there was a slight tremble in his wrist. The pink hammered against the baulk, and was caught in the jaws of the pocket. It remained there poised, unwilling to drop, refusing its master's desire. Vasagar straightened. His tone was cold and indifferent. 'You see, in life and in sport, perfection is difficult to obtain. And reasonableness . . . it is an attitude that is granted to few of us when under stress. I think it's time you left my home, now, Mr Spate.'

Charlie made no attempt to finish his drink before he left.

* * *

He drove back to headquarters in a sombre frame of mind. The visit to Vasagar's home had been a mistake; it had got him nowhere. On the other hand, he was certain that it was Vasagar who had set up the whole scenario. But using Charlie Spate was puzzling: it might have been down to pure malice, or an attempt to get Spate into trouble — because Vasagar knew well enough from past experience what Charlie Spate thought about him and his activities along the river. But where did Dieter Barschel fit into all this? Charlie still felt he could discover the answer if only he could find Romy Arendt. He gritted his teeth, remembering the feel of the woman, the scent of her . . . It had been a bad mistake, stupidity on his part. And yet, at the time . . .

His mind turned to Elaine Start. He knew that she was almost an obsession with him: he had made some clumsy advances in the past that had been rejected, sometimes with amusement, once with contempt. Yet he still felt a vague optimism about her even if he had perhaps spoiled his chances, by turning to another woman in frustration. But she was on his mind when he got back to the station. He wandered in, nodded to the duty officer. The thought occurred to him that he might use the excuse of her assigned operation on the counterfeiting ring to have a chat with her, maybe test the temperature of her feelings. 'DS Start around?'

The duty officer looked up from his newspaper. 'She's in the interview room.'

'Who's she got with her?'

'That solicitor. The guy who reported the killing last night.'

Charlie Spate stared at him. 'Killing? I've heard nothing about a killing. What's going on?'

The duty officer laid his newspaper aside. His features expressed a vague unease. 'The call didn't go out for you. DS Start was assigned to interview the guy. I think she did try to get hold of you, but your mobile was switched off, and you weren't at home.'

The Nocturne club again, he'd been at Nocturne. With his mobile switched off.

'So who's been topped now? Has the corpse been identified?'

The duty officer had the grace to look somewhat embarrassed. 'That Romanian guy we arrested a while back. Dieter Barschel.'

Charlie Spate felt as though there was a block of ice in his stomach. He walked stiffly down the corridor, stood outside the door of the interview room for half a minute. He could hear voices inside. At last, he pushed open the door, entered. Heads turned. Elaine Start, conducting the interview; stared stonily at him and after a moment the constable beside her said, for the purpose of the recording, 'DCI Spate has just entered the room.' He hesitated, then added the time of entry.

Eric Ward was seated in front of Elaine Start, darksuited, his arms folded over his chest. His features were impassive as he stared at Charlie; it was almost as though he failed to recognise him. Elaine Start turned back to face Ward as Charlie eased himself into a corner of the room, leaning against the wall to the right of the door.

'So,' she said, continuing with her interview; 'you had no particular reason to go up to the cottage.'

'None other than I was somewhat concerned,' Ward replied, 'because my client had not been in touch. As I explained, he had asked to be accommodated in a safe house, away from reporters, I had asked my ex-wife for permission to use the cottage, and I'd left him there, at his explicit request.

He explained he had some things to do, calls to make, and that he'd be in touch later. But I heard nothing from him. I had some time on my hands yesterday afternoon, so I drove up to see how he was getting on.' He glanced at Charlie, then looked away. 'I found him there in the kitchen, on his back, the shotgun at his side. My first thought was that he'd committed suicide.'

'We're still looking at that,' Elaine commented quietly. 'But these calls you say he was going to make . . . there's no telephone line to the cottage.'

'He told me he'd use his mobile.'

'Our preliminary search last night didn't turn up a mobile phone.'

'I wouldn't know about that. I removed nothing from the place. As soon as I found him, I called the police.'

'Did you see anyone else in the vicinity?'

Eric Ward shook his head. 'No.' He hesitated, contradicted himself. 'At least, a half mile or so away, on the hill, I passed a car parked near the cliff. No one inside, as far as I could make out. Walkers, I presumed. Nothing else; no one else.'

'In the cottage there were some signs of disturbance, as if someone had been looking around. What did Barschel take with him to the cottage?'

The solicitor shrugged vaguely. 'Not much. Some clothes and personal items he had thrown together into a holdall. And a second case, heavy. I don't know what was in it. Papers and books he told me. I didn't see it when I looked around.'

'No phone, no case,' Elaine Start said with a sigh. She glanced at her watch. 'Unless you've anything else to say, we'll leave it there for the moment—'

'When we get time of death,' Charlie interrupted, 'I imagine you'll be able to tell us where you were.'

'In court, probably,' Eric Ward replied coldly. 'I don't think Barschel had been long dead when . . . when I got there.'

Charlie was intrigued by the slight hesitation. Then he caught Elaine Start's annoyed, withering glance. He raised a hand in apology. She turned back to the solicitor.

'The statement you made earlier will have been typed up by now: Perhaps you'd sign it before you leave. There's no doubt we'll want to talk to you again. Meanwhile, if there's anything else that occurs to you, please get in touch with me. Thanks for your time, Mr Ward.'

The constable beside her murmured into the tape machine, switched off and stood up to escort Eric Ward from the interview room. The solicitor's glance held Charlie's for a brief moment, then he brushed past him and the door closed behind him. Charlie stayed where he was, leaning against the wall, hands in pockets. Elaine Start remained seated, turned her head to look at him. 'That was unnecessary.'

He shrugged, unabashed. 'You know Ward fairly well.'

'Our paths have crossed,' Charlie admitted sourly. He still had an account to settle with the man who had humiliated him in court.

Elaine Start frowned. 'I get the odd feeling he's holding something back. He rang in last night from the cottage. It's owned by his ex-wife. He told us what he'd found. He stayed there while we sent up a car. The scene of crime unit was set up late last night and the forensic team are still up there. Ward's been cooperative, as one might expect — he's a lawyer, after all, an ex-copper, so he knows the score. But I'm left with the odd feeling that he's not giving us all he knows.'

Charlie brushed the thought aside. The ice was still in his stomach. 'Why wasn't I given the call last night?'

Her glance was cool. 'I was asked to pick up the enquiry. I went up to the cottage last night with the scene of crime unit.'

'I'm the senior crime officer. I should have been informed. So I could take charge.'

'I was acting under orders,' she said stiffly, and rose to her feet. She had a magnificent bosom: he'd always been aware of that and it intruded upon his thoughts now.

'Orders or not—' he began thickly.

She stood facing him, head up, a little shorter than him, a defiant curl to her lip. 'I'm aware you're my senior officer. I tried to contact you last night, DCI Spate, to inform you of these developments. First, because, believe it or not, I'm loyal to my senior officers, and second, because I knew you'd have a personal stake in this business, since it was Barschel who got stiffed. But I couldn't raise you. *That's* why you weren't informed. If you'd had your mobile switched on . . .'

Nocturne. And then, this morning, the useless attempt to beard Vasagar in his home. Charlie swore under his breath. 'I was following up another line of enquiry.'

'That's your prerogative, *sir*,' Elaine Start replied coolly. 'Anyway, now you've been informed, and everything is straight, maybe I can get on with the investigation.'

'Where are you going now?'

'Down to the labs. A preliminary chat with the forensic people. Ward might have thought it was a suicide — though he cannot understand why Barschel may have wished to kill himself, or where the shotgun came from. It doesn't look that way to me, and I'm pretty certain the pathologist will give me an answer to that effect.'

'That he was murdered? I'll come with you.'

She hesitated. He could see that she was unwilling to agree, but there was rank he could pull on her right now, even if she was acting under orders from above. That could be sorted out later. 'I'm coming with you,' he insisted.

Before she could answer the door opened suddenly. The man standing in the doorway asked, 'What progress have you made? Elaine, you'd better come along to my room and give me a report because something else has just come up.' Half hidden by the door, Charlie stepped forward and then stopped. There was a brief silence. Assistant Chief Constable Jim Charteris stared at him, his mouth rigid with surprise.

'Spate! What the hell are you doing here?'

'I've just heard about the death of Dieter Barschel. I came in to hear part of the interview with Ward. In a situation like this, it's all hands to the pump—'

'No!' The voice was hard and decisive. 'You're not touching this case, Spate. I don't want you within a mile of it!'

Charlie scowled. 'I'm senior crime officer—'

Charteris interrupted venomously. 'And you're not touching this with a bargepole, Spate. Let me remind you what's been going on. You targeted the dead man, caused him to be charged with possession, and then failed to give straight answers to questions put to you at the preliminary hearing. The media have had a field day; the Chief's been under pressure and is putting pressure on me, I asked you if there was any truth in the rumours, the innuendoes that Ward raised in court, and you bloody well lied to me! Can you imagine what would happen now, if you were involved in the enquiry into the death of Dieter Barschel? Can you possibly imagine the headlines? It would all be dredged up again; there'd be speculations about inefficiency, a likely cover-up, they'd start digging deeper into the allegations made in Colonel Vaughan's preliminary hearing, the damned reporters would be sloshing around in the mud to find out whatever dirt they can come up with! No, you're not coming anywhere near this case, DCI Spate! DS Elaine Start will handle it initially; there'll be a review later, to see if we can bring in a more senior officer. But it won't be you!'

'I think you're making a mistake—'

'The mistake is that I took your word on trust, when I asked you about the drugs bust on Barschel. That's it, my friend. You lied to me, and I've had enough. And there's been a complaint about harassment! I'm making out a full report to the Chief Constable. In the meantime I'm suspending you from all duties, subject to a full enquiry.' Charteris glared at Charlie, malice in his eyes. 'You hear me, DCI Spate? *As of now, you're suspended!*'

There was just one overriding thought in Charlie's enraged mind.

Vasagar.

CHAPTER 7

Eric wondered whether the forensic investigation would find anything that would cast doubt on his story.

He was not too much concerned about evidence regarding time of death: it was not affected by his account of his movements. There was nothing to link his time of arrival at the cottage with the moments when Dieter Barschel had died. But it was another matter when it came to the question of whether Hannah Witt had left any signs of her presence at the cottage. It was an uncertainty that still caused him anxiety when he returned to his office after the interview by Elaine Start.

He had given her all the information he could apart from the fact that he had not been alone at the cottage when he had stumbled upon the body of Dieter Barschel. He could even now hardly believe that he had been persuaded to keep her out of the whole thing. At the cottage he had ushered her out of the kitchen and was in the yard outside, about to use his mobile to phone the police and inform them of his discovery, when she had put a hand on his arm to stop him.

'Wait! You must not do this. We must leave.' Her tone was urgent.

'My client is dead,' he snapped, amazed. 'I have to report this. It may be suicide, more likely murder, but I can't just walk away and do nothing about it.'

'We could leave,' she pleaded, 'and you could phone without giving your name. We need not be here; we need not be involved.'

Eric shook his head. 'It wouldn't work. They'd be able to trace the call from mobile records. And I'm a lawyer, Hannah. I can't run around breaking the law like that.' Even though there had been occasions, he reminded himself ruefully, when he had done just that, or at least sailed very close to the illegal wind.

She was distraught, panicked, urgent. Her fingers dug into his arm. Close to hysteria, she begged, 'Then let me get away first. It's important that I am not involved. I would be in danger . . . others would be in danger. Let me get away from here before you call the police.'

'What on earth are you talking about?' he demanded, taking her fiercely by the arm. 'This is nonsense. I have to make the call—'

She took a deep breath, in an effort to control her emotions. 'No,' she said firmly, recovering some of her self-assurance. 'I cannot tell you everything now, I must make some phone calls to London, but think. *Think*. I told you I wanted to talk to Dieter Barschel and one reason was that I knew he could be in danger of his life. And now he is dead.'

'Yes, but that's now a matter for the police—'

'The police!' Her tone was scornful. 'You think you are safe, calling the police? How was it that Dieter Barschel was first put in the limelight? From the accounts in the newspapers he was charged with drug trafficking — a charge he denied. And what did you show in the courtroom? That there are bad people in the police. That someone there was involved in bringing these charges against Barschel. You saved him from prison — where he might have suffered the fate of the man I told you about in Germany. And now he is dead, and you turn to them for assistance? That is the action of a crazy man.'

He stared at her, shaking his head. Her view of the police in the UK was distorted. 'I'm an ex-policeman myself. There is some corruption among officers, I know that, but what you're hinting at cannot be right.' He took her by the arms, gently shaking her. 'There are things here you're not telling me. Did you know Barschel personally? You told me you wanted to interview him about his past. What do you know about his history? All I know is he was once a footballer, who got involved in petty crime when he was down on his luck. And now he's dead. What do you know about him? Why is he dead?'

She shook her head again, lowering her eyes in desperation. 'There's someone I must talk to. He will know what to do. But if I am trapped here with you, if I am questioned by the police, I will lose my chance — perhaps I have already lost it now. This is important to me. But while I can still seek the answers, while I can still go on . . . the police come, they find me here, I will be caught, exposed, and then perhaps my own life will be in danger. You must get me away.' She lifted her head, and the green eyes were clouded with desperate tears. 'Please, Mr Ward. I beg you.'

She was younger than he; she was beautiful; she was terrified. These must have been the reasons for what he then decided. It was a decision he was still mulling over in his mind, in his office.

'All right,' he had said, shaking his head in doubt. 'I'll get you away, on condition that when I pick you up again you tell me just what the hell this is all about. There's no real reason why you should be involved in this anyway. I'll get you away, and I won't tell the police that you were here. But after that . . .'

He had worked it all out quickly. He could not afford to waste too much time: he would have to phone the police from the cottage and be there when they arrived. There wasn't sufficient time to take her back to Newcastle, where he understood she had rented an apartment. It would have to be somewhere closer.

He bundled her into the car; she was almost shaking with relief. As he turned the Celica in the yard the dying sun glared on his windscreen; as the car lurched into the stone track there was a gleam of light from the distant hill. He drove quickly. They did not speak, and Hannah huddled against the car door, arms crossed, clutching her own shoulders, shuddering occasionally. They crossed the craggy hill; as they drove past the crag itself he glanced to where the walkers' car had been parked but it had gone. Then they were bouncing their way over cattle grids and into wild, high country. They dropped into the wide dale with its hard-working river, past old spoil heaps that were now turning into flower-rich grass-land and short heath. Eric swung into a back road, crossed the railway line and in a little while they caught sight of Stanhope below them. He glanced at his watch: they'd made good time. A left turn took them over the river by way of the medieval Stanhope Bridge and into Stanhope itself.

He found a parking place in the Market Square under the back wall of Stanhope Castle, reputed to have been built at such cost that it ruined the builder in 1798. He told Hannah to stay in the car; she nodded acquiescence. He walked along past the fortified manor house called Stanhope Hall on the small rise above Stanhope Burn, past the ancient brew house and corn mill and the modern buildings of the Dales Centre.

The small hotel — the Bonny Moor Hen — seemed suitable for his purpose. He walked into reception; the plump young receptionist was swift to help. There was certainly a single room available for a young lady. It would be required for one night, possibly two. Eric gave his credit card number and told her he would account for the bill. When he got back to the car Hannah was still huddled in her seat, wiping her eyes. She had recovered much of her composure, but there was still a haunting anxiety in her eyes. He slid into the driving seat beside her. He was forced to wait before he could leave the Market Square as a big dark Mercedes with tinted windows partly blocked his way. When he pulled out and headed for the hotel he said, 'I've booked you a room.

I'll be back tomorrow evening, or the following morning. Put anything you want on the hotel account. Stay close to the hotel; don't wander about.'

She nodded, saying nothing. Eric stopped outside the main entrance of the hotel, watched her as she went inside, then reversed the Celica into a side street, cursing as the tourists in the car with tinted windows drove slowly past. Time was precious. He pulled out at last, drove back the way he had come, out of the wide valley of Weardale and back up over the quarry-scattered landscape.

He had promised her he would return to collect her as soon as he could. He had made the call to the police from the cottage. He had awaited their arrival. He had waited there with them, answering their questions, until the forensic team had arrived, and he had been allowed to drive back to Newcastle. And next day, as requested, he had turned up at the station for an interview with DS Elaine Start. Once it was over he returned to his office on the Quayside where he checked his diary, made a few calls, asked Susie to cancel a few appointments with prospective clients, telling her he would not be available for the rest of the day. She clucked a motherly tongue at him before agreeing to carry out his instructions. She arched an eyebrow, shook her head at him as he hurried out. He smiled to himself: she really had his best interests at heart. He wondered what she would have said if she'd known what he was doing for the attractive young girl she had met briefly in his office.

It was late afternoon when he returned to Stanhope. He hesitated about where he should park the car, but finally decided to use the hotel car park, rather than the Market Square.

It was not the same receptionist he had met earlier. She smiled pleasantly as he approached her. 'Would you call Miss Hannah Witt in her room, please.'

'Miss Witt?' The smile faded on the girl's face. She was plump, wide-eyed and now somewhat flustered. 'She . . . I . . . You'd better have a word with the manager.' She rose hastily and vanished into the back room behind the reception desk. He heard voices engaged in a low, hurried discussion. He felt a slow crawling of anxiety at the back of his neck. The man who came out from the back room was about sixty, balding, narrow-featured and anxious.

'My name is Grant. I'm the hotel manager. May I ask who you are, sir?'

'Ward. I want to see Miss Witt. She'll be checking out now. You already have my credit card details. If you'll make out the bill, and call Miss Witt . . .' He took out his wallet, extracted his credit card.

The manager seemed transfixed. The anxiety in the pouched eyes had grown. 'I . . . er . . . You clearly haven't heard. Miss Witt has already been checked out. That is . . . well, I'm sorry to say she was involved in an accident last night.'

'Accident? What happened?' Eric asked, startled.

The manager rubbed a hand anxiously over his jaw. 'It was about nine o'clock last night. I wasn't on duty . . . my wife . . . It seems Miss Witt wanted to make a phone call. She wouldn't use the phone in her room. Perhaps it was because she thought our charges were expensive, but really, I assure you we don't charge any more than is usual in family hotels such as ours. So it wasn't really our fault, was it?' He gasped a half sigh of regret.

'Never mind that,' Eric snapped brusquely. 'What about this accident?'

'It was a hit and run, just outside the hotel. As far as I understand,' Mr Grant averred, scratching nervously at his cheek, 'Miss Witt asked at reception and Molly told her she could use the room telephone but she said no so Molly said there was a phone box down the street so Miss Witt thanked her and then she went out. That's when it happened. Mr Carsholt, who runs the newspaper shop down the street, caught a glimpse of it. This car just hit her as she was crossing the street outside the hotel. Mr Carsholt had seen her leaving the building. He phoned for an ambulance straight away. They came quite quickly, I assure you.'

'How badly hurt was she?' Eric demanded.

The hotel manager flicked a pink tongue over regretful lips. 'I'm sorry to tell you she had severe head injuries. She's been taken to hospital in Durham.'

'That's a hell of a way,' Eric snarled in frustration.

'They have the facilities . . . The way the hospital service works these days . . .' The manager's voice died away uncertainly. He peered at Eric with sad, sympathetic eyes. 'Mrs Grant and I, we extend our sympathies, and we're sure she'll be all right. In the circumstances please forget about the bill.'

Eric stared at him, unseeing. His mind whirled with the way she had panicked, her anxiety about getting away from the cottage.

'May I . . . may I ask what your relationship with Miss Witt may be?' the manager asked timidly. 'Are you family . . . or just a friend?'

'I'm her solicitor,' Eric snapped, not quite accurately.

A certain relief entered Mr Grant's manner. He sighed gustily. 'Ah, well that means there shouldn't be any harm in it.'

'What are you talking about?' Eric asked irritably, his mind elsewhere.

'Well, the ambulance, when it came with the paramedics, they picked her up from the road you see and it was urgent so off they roared into the night . . . and well, they didn't pick up her things. Not that there was much. We wondered about that,' he added, curiosity creeping into his tone. 'Anyway, it was just her handbag. Nothing else, even though she was booked in for possibly two nights. How she was going to manage about clothes . . .' Seeing the look in Eric's eyes he continued hastily, 'Anyway, if you're her solicitor, I think it's best to release her effects to you. I'm sure you agree it would be best if you signed for them . . .'

Back in the Celica Eric sat dumbly for a while, unable to think clearly. He cast his mind back over events: the lonely cottage, the dead man, his head blown off with a shotgun, the terrified girl. And then, almost unbidden, the recollection of a gleam of light, a flash on the distant crag, and a car with tinted windows, sliding past him as he prepared to return to the cottage . . .

He picked up Hannah Witt's handbag. There was little in it, apart from a few personal effects and her purse. He opened it. It contained some notes, a set of keys, tagged with an address. And three credit cards. He stared at them, uncomprehending.

Each card bore the name Hannah Guderian.

CHAPTER 8

DCI Charlie Spate, for the present moment feeling sorry for himself, and very unemployed, reached a decision.

It was not a decision that appealed to him but after two days kicking his heels in his apartment, brooding at the injustice of it all, cursing Assistant Chief Constable Charteris, curbing his instinctive desire to get after Mark Vasagar and beat the hell out of him, and spending his evenings in the pub in morose drinking bouts, he felt he had to do something.

He was still convinced of the sequence of events that had led to his suspension. In his wilder moments he told himself that if only Elaine Start had been prepared to enter a relationship with him all this would never have happened but grudgingly he was finally forced to recognise that no blame could really be laid at her door. This was not the first time he had taken advantage of the opportunities offered to him by his job: he'd been stupid before. It was one of the reasons he'd been advised to leave the Met. Relationships with the people on the shady side of the street, that could lead to conflict with the demands of his duties . . .

But as far as his suspension was concerned, he was certain Mark Vasagar was behind it all: for reasons he had yet to discover, Charlie Spate had been set up over the Dieter

Barschel business. The girl who was used to trigger it had disappeared; Vasagar had denied involvement and then used his contacts to put more heat on Charlie Spate; Charteris had complied when Vasagar had complained of harassment in his own home, and now Charlie was out of the frame. But up to now Charlie could detect no direct link between Vasagar and Dieter Barschel. And the thing somehow didn't make sense: why had Barschel been targeted with a drugs plant — Charlie had to admit to himself now that it had been a plant — and what was the necessity thereafter to murder the man when Ward had obtained his release?

Ward. Charlie had considered the matter for hours. He had thought of contacting Elaine, to see if there was anything she could suggest, but she had her hands full with the killing, and there was still that counterfeiting business that she was supposed to be handling for Charteris. Half-grown solutions appeared from time to time in Charlie's mind, to be replaced by others until they were all swirling around inside his head to no effect. It was when he realised that he was getting nowhere that he decided he had to face the one person was seemed to have some central role to play in the business. The thought stuck in his throat for a long time before he decided that there was nothing else he could do but turn to Eric Ward.

The solicitor's secretary had the usual frosty look in her eye when he appeared at the Quayside office. She made no secret of her dislike for Charlie Spate: it might be the feeling in most secretaries that they wanted to protect the man who employed them; it might have been something more personal. Charlie cared nothing about that.

'Is he in?' he growled, uncompromisingly.

Susie Cartwright sniffed her disapproval. 'Mr Ward has a client with him.'

'I'll wait,' Charlie announced and slumped into a chair. Susie Cartwright turned her back on him and continued typing, her back stiff with resentment. Not a bad-looking woman he considered, bit old for Charlie Spate, but she was wearing well. He'd heard a rumour that there was a guy in the Lord Chancellor's Department who had a fancy for her — a loser probably. Charlie cleared his throat and glanced at his watch impatiently.

After a few minutes the door to the solicitor's office opened and a man backed out, raising a hand in thanks. As he turned he caught sight of Charlie Spate. His eyes widened and his mouth dropped open.

'Hello, Bellini,' Charlie hailed him cheerfully. 'So when did they let you out? You talking to the lawyers now to set up cover for a new scam?'

The big man they called Bull Bellini closed the door, ducked his head and backed away from Charlie, crossing the room quickly. He was not too bright a character, Charlie reckoned; mainly muscle, and didn't have the sense to cover his tracks when he worked with more cunning men. He was the one who usually got caught in the bag, but Charlie had to admit he was loyal. He'd never snitched on anyone. It was a bit frustrating for the police, really: some felt a little bit sorry for the big man.

Ward's office door reopened as Bellini vanished down the stairway. Eric Ward stood there, looking at Charlie. He said nothing, glanced at his secretary, then shrugged and turned back into his room. He left the door open. Charlie took it as permission to enter. 'We'll be a while,' he remarked to Susie Cartwright as he walked past her desk. She ignored him completely.

Eric Ward was seated behind his desk. His body language suggested to Charlie that the visit was not a welcome one. 'Mind if I take a seat?' Charlie asked pleasantly.

Ward waved a hand dismissively. There was a resentful curl to his lips. He folded his arms across his chest and held Charlie's gaze steadily. 'I suppose this is about Dieter Barschel.'

'Who else?'

'You'll already be aware that I've been interviewed, given a statement about the killing. I've done all I can to help. There's nothing more I can give you.'

'I'm not so certain about that,' Charlie replied carefully. He fell silent, his eyes fixed upon the solicitor. What he was about to say was difficult; it went very much against the grain that he should explain himself, give Ward personal information, admit to weakness and stupidity. But there was no other option open to him if he was to get to the bottom of what was going on.

Something of his uncertainty communicated itself to the solicitor. Ward frowned, watching Charlie's features, a stain of suspicion in his eyes. 'What is it you want from me, Mr Spate?'

The word stuck a while in Charlie's throat but he finally got it out. 'Assistance.' He thought of another difficult word, then used it. 'Cooperation.'

Slowly, Ward said, 'I don't understand. I have already cooperated with the police as far as I can. I don't see—'

Charlie took a deep breath. 'All right, cards on the table. I've been suspended from duty.'

Eric Ward raised his eyebrows in surprise. 'I hadn't heard that.'

Charlie grunted. 'Well, it's a fact. And it's partly down to you. You stiffed me in that preliminary hearing.'

'I was doing what I could for my client,' Ward responded coldly.

'Where did you get your information?' Charlie demanded.

'I can't tell you that.'

'How much do you really know about it all?' Charlie asked suspiciously, after a short silence.

Eric Ward hesitated, clearly considering the question carefully. 'I assume you're talking about the death of Barschel, rather than why you've been suspended.'

'To some extent, it's all part of the same thing,' Charlie admitted.

Eric Ward was surprised by the admission. He thought about it for a while, watching Charlie carefully. Then he shrugged. 'All right. I don't quite know how this helps you with your problems, Mr Spate, but Dieter Barschel is dead now; so I suppose I can admit that much of my defence was . . . tactically inspired. All I had was rumour. No actual proof. There were whispers around town, I had a woman's name. By raising the questions I did I hoped that I'd cause the kind of flurry at your headquarters that would cause them to drop the trumped-up charges against Dieter Barschel. The tactic succeeded. But it was a gamble.'

'And one that screwed me. So you had no proofs you could take to a full trial.'

'And I didn't have much expectation of getting Romy Arendt to testify. I couldn't even find her.'

'That makes two of us,' Charlie Spate snarled angrily. He glared at the solicitor. 'You're a cold bastard, Ward.'

He could see that Ward was thinking it takes one to know one. 'I do my job as I see it. And I fight fire with fire. You and I both know the drugs arrest was a set-up. But that's yesterday's news. Dieter Barschel is dead. I've moved on. So should you.'

Charlie leaned back in his chair. There was an odd note in Ward's voice. Something was bothering him. And it could be something to do with Dieter Barschel. Charlie chewed over the thought in his mind. But he'd already made the decision. It was time he went through with it.

'I don't like you, Ward.'

'I reciprocate the feeling.'

'I don't like you, but I find myself facing a dilemma. I can't just move on, as you suggest. I've got problems. I'm facing an enquiry, I'm suspended, and I feel I'm being hung out to dry.'

'Maybe you should get yourself a lawyer,' Ward replied sarcastically.

'That's what I've decided to do,' Charlie said, and after a short silence he added, 'You'. He saw the protest starting to rise and held up a hand. 'No. Hear me out. I've no intention of asking you to represent me. It's humiliation enough that I'm coming to you at all. To ask for help.'

Ward clearly recognised the difficulty that Charlie Spate must have faced in coming to the Quayside office. He shook his head regretfully. 'I've already told you I don't see how I—'

'I want us to put our heads together to find out what the hell is going on,' Charlie interrupted sharply. 'We work together; we trade information; we come clean with each other. Your client's been killed. My guess is you want to find out why as much as I do.'

There was a short silence. Initially taken aback, Eric Ward now seemed to have calmed, was considering the matter with care. At last, he said, 'You'll forgive me for expressing the thought that I can't be sure you'd ever come clean with me, Mr Spate. Suspended and in disgrace or not.'

Charlie's mouth twisted. 'Then I'll show you my good faith. I'll tell you just what happened in that drugs business. You've heard rumours. I'll tell you exactly what happened.'

Ward leaned forward. 'That's up to you. But a warning. You're not my client, Mr Spate. What's to prevent me giving out anything you tell me to others, to your detriment?'

'The hell with that,' Charlie snapped. 'I told you. This is to show my good faith. I want us to work together to our mutual benefit.'

Eric Ward shrugged, said nothing, but there was curiosity in his eyes.

'It all started a few months back,' Charlie admitted. 'We all know who used to control a large part of the organised crime along the river, and we all know just who's taken over the business, albeit more quietly, and more subtly. Which makes it more difficult to pin the bastard down. You'll know who I'm talking about.'

'I know you have a thing about Mark Vasagar,' Ward agreed quietly.

Charlie nodded. 'I like to keep the pressure on, make it known that I'm around, that we're keeping an eye on things. Several of us work a routine. Mine involved dropping in at one of Vasagar's nightclubs, Nocturne. Have a drink, see who's coming and going. And one night . . . well, all right, I was feeling a bit down, and a bit horny, and I met this girl in the bar. We got into conversation. She knew all along I was the fuzz, but she was pleasant, a little bit distant. She didn't exactly throw herself at me, but we got along. And after a while, I got to visiting her at her apartment.'

'Romy Arendt.'

Charlie took a deep breath. 'I knew she was a hooker, of course. But she was . . . interesting. I knew she was on the game, but at the time I got the impression that she was straight. This wasn't commercial. I didn't get involved, like, but it was pretty good and I felt good about it. And of course we talked.'

'The inevitable pillow talk,' Ward commented drily.

Charlie managed a cynical laugh. 'Crazy, isn't it? An experienced copper like me and I fall for an old trick like that. There we were wrigglin' around in bed and she tells me she's got a problem. She's being bothered by an ex-lover. And he'd knocked her about a bit when they were together. He wanted to renew the relationship. She didn't want that. She asks me if there's anything I can do to help. And at that particular moment I'd do *anything* to help, you know what I mean? Of course, when I cooled down I was changing my mind, but I was also curious. She said no more, but I'd caught the bait. I asked her more about this guy. She told me his name. She told me he was into drug peddling. And she told me she was scared of him.' Charlie thought back over the events of that time. 'Now, I think she was scared of someone else, not Dieter Barschel.'

'So what happened then?' Ward asked.

'I raised it with her again. She said that Barschel was dealing, and he worked the racetracks. She gave me details and I thought, hey, what's wrong with using this information and making an arrest? I wasn't going to get involved myself, but I got three officers to do the job. They had to wait until they saw the package passing, and then they could pounce.'

Eric Ward frowned. 'Didn't you query the idea? I mean, passing drugs at the racetrack?'

'Hey, villains get up to all sorts of stuff! They can be really stupid, you know that. Anyway, we went ahead with it, and the lads did the job.'

'What about the man passing the package? So he wasn't a plant you set up?'

Charlie Spate shook his head. 'Romy gave me a time and place, but he wasn't our man. We recognised him later as a small-time grafter, but I told the lads to leave him alone, concentrate on Barschel. Then it all blew up in my face, with the defence you put up. As soon as the CCTV footage was hauled into play, and you were given the woman's name, I was in trouble. That's why I was in court to be questioned: it was made clear to me that I had to front up, not any of the lads who made the arrest.'

'And now?' the solicitor asked quietly.

'I got suckered by Romy Arendt, but I know it was her employer Vasagar who was behind it. Now I want to know why Vasagar set up Barschel in the way he did. And I want to know why Barschel got killed.'

'You're *convinced* it was Vasagar behind this?' Ward asked doubtfully.

'Hell, she worked in his club! It stands out a mile.'

Charlie waited. Eric Ward rose from his chair and prowled around the room uneasily, thinking over what Charlie had told him. Charlie guessed what he had said merely amounted to confirmation of suspicions the solicitor had himself held — indeed, Ward had already admitted that he would have faced difficulties proving the issues he had raised before the magistrate. And he could tell that Ward was uncertain . . . but he was also left with the feeling that he had struck another, separate chord with the man. At last Eric Ward took a deep breath, and nodded. He stood facing Charlie. 'All right, Spate. I'll take you on trust. I'll take you at your word. You're right, I want to find out what's been going on. It seems to have become personal for you, now you've been suspended. Well, for me it's become a personal issue too.' He hesitated. 'The statement I made to DS Start wasn't the whole truth. The truth is, I wasn't alone when I found Dieter Barschel.'

'What?' Charlie started.

'There was a young woman with me. I took her to Stanhope, went back to the cottage, then phoned the police.'

'What the hell did you do that for?' Charlie demanded.

Ward ignored the question. 'After making the statement I went back for her. But she'd been taken to hospital. Hit and run.'

Charlie shook his head. 'I don't follow you. I don't understand what's happening here . . . You stuck out your neck for this girl . . .'

'I'd better explain,' the solicitor said grimly.

* * *

He had called at the hospital and had a brief consultation with the doctor in charge of the case. He was a clean-shaven, earnest young man, who didn't look older than fifteen, with deeply serious eyes. 'I'm afraid you can't speak with her — you can see her if you wish, but she'll be unable to communicate with you. She's in intensive care at the moment and she'll be kept in a chemically induced coma there, to rest the brain. We'll use steroids to ease the swelling, and barbiturates to keep her unconscious. She'll also be paralysed with muscle anaesthetics so she'll stay immobile until her brain recovers.' He frowned. 'With cerebral oedema, well, one has to be vigilant, to prevent the swelling of the brain from pushing down on its stem.' He eyed Eric doubtfully. 'We don't actually have an identity . . . you say you're her solicitor, so I presume you can tell us her name. For purposes of record, you understand. The ambulance people, they were a bit hasty. Understandably, in the circumstances.'

'Her name is Hannah . . .' Eric had hesitated. 'Hannah Guderian.'

'I'd be grateful if you could give her address to the nurse on reception. You want to see her now?'

She was in a private ward. It was as the young doctor had explained. Her eyes were closed, her face bruised, her head swathed in bandages. She was lying very still. A cold anger coursed through Eric's body.

Outside the hospital he took out the keys he had found in her purse. He looked again at the address. He thought once more of going to the police, but he was reluctant. He would have to explain about making a false statement; he could not be sure what had really happened in Stanhope; he was shaken by the fact that she had given him a false name — or alternatively, that she was carrying someone else's credit cards. But more than anything, it was the thought of the young woman lying in the hospital bed, deliberately run down. His anger simmered inside him: he wanted to know.

He drove to the address on the key tag. It was a four-storeyed Victorian house that would have once been home to a professional man with a large family and servants accommodated on the top floor. The street was quiet, an upmarket residential area in Gosforth. Most of the houses in the street, like this one, had been turned into apartments, owners cashing in on the property boom. He parked the car at the end of the street, walked back under the pollarded lime trees that shaded the road. He checked the address box at the portico: the key tag was designated for the ground floor but there was no name on the ground-floor apartment slot. He used the first key to open the Yale lock on the front door. The hallway was cool and quiet, the floor Victorian-tiled. His shoes sent echoes up the stairwell as he crossed to the apartment door.

Inside everything was very tidy. There was a table just inside the door. He picked up the letters placed there: mainly junk mail, but one was a brief letter of confirmation of rental from the owner of the apartment. The girl had taken a one-month rental. She had not intended staying long on Tyneside.

He glanced around at the sitting room. It was gloomy; the heavy curtains over the tall windows were still drawn. He looked briefly into the kitchen but there was little sign of use. Clearly, the young woman who lay silent in the hospital had barely used the apartment. He walked through to the bedroom. There was a suitcase beside the bed. He flipped open the lid; it was empty apart from a few items of discarded clothing. On the table underneath the window there was a laptop computer. Eric hesitated, then sat down on the chair in front of the machine, opened it up. It was security-barred. For a while he played around with it, seeking a possible password — Witt, Guderian, Hannah, and various combinations — but he soon gave up: he needed an expert to break into these files. He did not possess the necessary skills.

He went across to the wardrobe, and found clothes hanging there. Hesitantly, he went through them. He became vaguely aware of a light perfume. It reminded him of the injured woman and a stab of anger surged through him once more. In the pocket of a jacket he found an address book. It was small. It contained a few telephone numbers but no addresses.

One of the numbers had a London STD code.

* * *

'So that's all you found?' Charlie Spate asked, slumped in the chair in Eric's office. 'It's not much to go on. There was nothing that might explain why she was using a false name? Nothing that might explain why she wanted to talk to Dieter Barschel? Or why she was panicked at the thought of staying at the cottage with you?'

Eric shook his head. 'No.'

Charlie scratched at his cheek in frustration. 'You say she was scared of going to the police. What the hell was that all about?'

Eric grimaced. 'I got the impression she didn't trust them. Maybe it was because of her experiences in the past, in Germany. Or maybe it was something else. After all, she was aware that the arrest of Barschel was trumped up. With police involvement. Perhaps that was why she was reluctant to be found at the cottage.'

Charlie humphed, uncomfortably aware of the part he had played in the affair. 'So we've got nowhere further.'

'Not quite,' Eric disagreed. 'She asked me to get her away from the cottage, to avoid the attentions of the police.

But she also promised that she would explain everything to me later. After she had spoken to someone in London. And at the hotel, she had deliberately avoided using the hotel phone. She got knocked down when she was heading for a public phone box.'

'If she had used the hotel phone, the call could easily have been traced, from hotel records,' Charlie mused.

'There's only one phone number with a London code in her address book. But no address. The telephone companies won't give a name and address if you just give them a phone number.'

'I'm a copper,' Charlie grunted. 'They'll give it to me.' There was a short pause. Eric held Charlie Spate's glance. 'I was thinking of going down to find out whose number this might be.'

Charlie grinned sourly. 'I was thinking just the same thing. After all, it's about the only lead we've got.' He rose from his seat, clearly happier now that he felt there was something active he could do. 'Me and you, it's an unholy combination, I'm sure you'll agree, but I think it's a good idea if we both go. For me, it's an old stamping ground. I'll be able to show you the sights!'

CHAPTER 9

Eric hated flying. The medication he used normally kept at bay the effects of glaucoma but every time he took a flight, on take-off the old familiar pains returned, cat claws scratching at the back of his eyes, shudders of excruciating agony shooting through his skull. He was aware of the curious glance Charlie Spate cast at him as he put his head back in the seat, closed his eyes, but he said nothing, and in an effort to forget the pain Eric concentrated upon the irony of his position. An officer of the court who had lied to the police, embarking upon a clandestine adventure with a police officer under suspension, breaking all the rules, getting involved in dangerous waters, and alongside a man he disliked intensely.

There had been other occasions when they had crossed paths, other occasions when Charlie Spate had held an edge over him, knew something to his discredit but had stayed his hand for purposes of his own. At one point there had been a degree of respect between them, if not liking, but even that had gone now. They were warring tigers in the same cage, and he had no doubt Charlie Spate would rend him if he felt it necessary, but he was forced to admit that he held the same feelings about the policeman. They had different objectives in mind, different motivations, but for the moment they were tied loosely together in their search for answers.

Why had Dieter Barschel died, and who had tried to kill Hannah Guderian?

Hannah Witt. Hannah Guderian.

The flight to Heathrow was just over one hour.

The two men took the train into Central London. They said little to each other. It seemed that true to his word, DCI Spate had had little trouble in obtaining an address to match the phone number. He had simply identified himself and said he was in the process of investigating a crime. When they reached King's Cross Charlie hailed a black cab. The driver eyed them, sitting in silence in the back of the cab, and clearly decided, against his normal inclinations, not to engage them in conversation.

Eric paid off the driver at the Tube station entrance. Charlie Spate gestured towards the road crossing. 'It'll be just down there, Mill Road, maybe two hundred yards,' he announced. They walked side by side: the row of nineteenth-century terraced houses leered at them blankly, curtained windows, stained facades, tiny mean gardens barred by walls and low iron gates. A few of the gardens demonstrated attempts to grow ornamental shrubs; the attempts were forlorn, the shrubs curling their leaves in untended desperation. There was an air of desolation about the whole street, but Eric had no doubt that the house prices would be high compared with those in the north. The house they wanted was a little smarter than many; the windows and door had recently been painted, the front garden had been laid with stone, through which weeds struggled weakly.

The house had clearly been let out in three flats: Eric hated to think how little room there would be in the garret at the top. He rang the lowest of the three bells. They could hear the sound echoing within; it died away into a protracted silence. Eric tried the bell again. This time there was a muffled response from within the building. They waited.

Finally the door opened; the man's head was at their waist level. He was about sixty years of age, and he was in a wheelchair. His hair was thin, short-cropped, and grey, his stubbly chin unshaven. He had pushed his spectacles up on his forehead; below them was a frown of suspicion. Perhaps that came from living in this part of London. He wore faded jeans and a cardigan that had seen better days. On his feet were brocaded slippers. He looked his visitors up and down, with a puzzled air, but when he spoke his tone was not unfriendly and it was relatively cultured. Eric could not place the accent.

'Can I help you?'

'My name is Ward. I'm a solicitor.'

The sharp eyes held his for a few moments, then glanced towards Eric's companion. Charlie Spate opened his mouth to identify himself then thought better of it. He remained silent.

The man in the wheelchair grunted. 'My rent's been paid up to date, so I can't imagine why the landlord would set a lawyer on me.' He glanced again at Charlie Spate. 'He's not a bailiff is he? The quiet one?'

'I'm not a bailiff,' Charlie asserted sharply. 'Your name is Saville?'

The man shook his head. 'Wrong man. That's the name of the landlord. Miserable bugger he is, too. But I'm the tenant here. Have been for years. Jacobsen. Karl Jacobsen. If you want Saville, just wait a moment and I'll give you his address.'

'No,' Eric said quickly. 'It'll be you we want to talk to. The man who lives here.'

'That'll be me, right enough. So what can I do for you gentlemen?'

'We'd like to talk with you about Hannah Guderian,' Eric said. 'She's been injured. She's in a hospital in Newcastle.'

There was a long silence as Jacobsen stared at them blankly. Then he gave a long slow hiss between his teeth. He stayed still, then gave a slow, sad shake of the head, opened the door wider, backed away in his wheelchair. 'You'd better come in. Close the door behind you. There are young buggers in the next street who are always causing trouble. Police never do a thing about it.'

They followed him along the narrow passageway towards the back of the house. He turned into the sitting room. It was sparsely furnished but the chairs were of a good quality. There was an oak table in one corner of the room: a computer was placed squarely upon it, some reference books stacked to one side. Jacobsen cocked his head towards the PC. 'I may be in a wheelchair, but I can still make a reasonable sort of living. Journalism. Not big time these days, but once . . .'

He gestured to them to take seats. Eric sat on the settee, Spate in a worn leather easy chair. Jacobsen swung his wheelchair to face them. His face seemed tired, his pouched eyes weary. 'So she's been hurt.' He shook his head. 'I warned her it could be dangerous.'

'She was involved in a hit and run accident.'

'So are you looking into compensation, or what? A solicitor, and a . . .' Jacobsen's voice died away as he regarded Spate. 'Compensation?' Eric hesitated. 'Have you heard of Dieter Barschel?'

Jacobsen raised his eyebrows, regarded Eric quietly for several seconds then nodded, ran a hand across his eyes.

'Was it you who suggested she seek him out?'

Jacobsen permitted himself a sad smile. 'I did not. I warned her against it. But she was determined. One argues helplessly against that level of determination.'

'When she first came to me,' Eric commented, 'she told me she was called Hannah Witt. Why would she do that? I discovered her real surname was Guderian — after she'd been run down.'

The old man's eyes widened. 'Did she do that? Ha . . .' He nodded. 'It underlies her search for the truth. She was the daughter of a second marriage. She had a half-sister: Andrea Witt.'

'That doesn't really explain anything,' Eric suggested. Jacobsen took a long, shuddering breath. 'Andrea Witt was a journalist, in Germany. I met her several times: she was a good writer. Dogged in her search for the truth. Her half-sister would seem to possess the same characteristic.'

'Hannah Guderian?' Eric recalled their first meeting: it was he who had assumed she was a reporter. She had gone along with that belief, for her own purposes, and perhaps almost instinctively had used the Witt name. A journalist.

'She adopted her half-sister's identity;' Charlie muttered.

'So you have a tongue, my friend,' Jacobsen smiled. 'Yes, that would seem to be the case. Hannah Guderian is the younger half-sister of Andrea Witt, a successful journalist. She wrote regularly for *Bild* and other papers. Until about a year ago, when Andrea disappeared.'

There was a short silence, where each man was occupied with his own thoughts. 'Why did Hannah come to you?' Eric asked at last.

Jacobsen sighed. 'My name would have appeared in Andrea Witt's files, as a contact, a person interested in the issues she was working on. Hannah became obsessed with trying to find out what happened to her beloved older half-sister. She worshipped her, you know; She spent months following up files that Andrea had kept, and when she had obtained much of the picture she came to me, because of what I also had written, in the old days.'

'About what? About Dieter Barschel?'

Jacobsen shook his head. 'Not directly.'

'So what was her interest in Barschel? Did he have anything to do with the disappearance of Andrea Witt?' Charlie Spate asked.

'Ha, you go too fast, my friend. No, I doubt if Barschel ever met Andrea Witt. No, Hannah wanted to talk to Barschel because she saw him as a link in the chain.'

'What chain?' Charlie Spate asked harshly. There was something in his tone that caught Jacobsen's attention. He eyed Charlie carefully for a few moments before he replied.

'It is a chain that stretches back many years.' He shook his head. 'It is sometimes thought that all of East Germany's dark secrets have now been revealed. But that is not so. Certainly, Andrea Witt did not believe so. For some three years she had been pressurising the German authorities to reopen investigations into at least ten suspicious deaths . . . Ten, maybe more . . .'

Eric stiffened. He recalled Hannah's early remarks to him when she was trying to obtain Barschel's address. She had talked of mysterious deaths, killings, disappearances. 'Hannah told me something about a man suffocated in his cell before he took part in a spy swap,' Eric said thoughtfully. 'And another unsolved case . . .'

Jacobsen straightened in his wheelchair. 'I've no doubt you will both have heard of the secret police in East Germany.'

'The Stasi,' Spate muttered.

'That is so. I myself have good reason to remember them,' Jacobsen said with a tired smile, caressing his left leg. 'I spent three months in their tender care. But I am still here, and lucky to be alive, even if I have a smashed hip, and have lost one leg. I sometimes use an artificial limb, but even after all these years I find it difficult, so at home . . .' He collected his thoughts again. 'Andrea Witt was following up a story when she disappeared. She claimed to have discovered the existence of a state-sponsored assassination squad that had been operating in East Germany in the years before reunification. She wrote several articles about it. *Tagesspiegel* in Berlin ran several of her bylines. I have copies of them on file. She claimed that the unit, which might have been part of Stasi, or maybe of the army, was an East German death squad, working with one hundred per cent logistical support from politicians in the German Democratic Republic, the DDR. The story was followed up in *Bild,* the mass circulation tabloid, until it gradually faded in the face of other sensations . . . But Miss Witt had a true journalistic nose: she sniffed cover-up and corruption, and she would not let go.'

'But at the reunification of Germany, surely such a squad would have been disbanded,' Charlie Spate argued.

Jacobsen held up a dissenting hand. 'Rats leave sinking ships but they have a capacity for swimming to safe havens. Let's be clear here. The death squad that Andrea Witt was exposing had as its function the murder of those people who had been deemed by the authorities to have committed acts of treason against the state. Or those suspected of preparing to do *so*. Indeed, they would kill anyone whose actions might cast the DDR in a harsh light. Cheaper than state trials,' he added cynically. 'You know; it's interesting that nowadays Germany is going through a wave of nostalgia for things East German — it is dubbed *Ostalgie* with colourful television shows featuring former DDR sports stars talking wistfully about East German pop music! People forget . . . but Miss Witt did not. And then she disappeared.'

'I repeat,' Charlie said stubbornly. 'When the state collapsed, surely the death squads were finished.'

'Or changed their function,' Jacobsen replied, staring thoughtfully again at Spate. 'The thesis that Miss Witt was working on contended that the animal changed its colour but was still very much alive. It was too effective an arm merely to disappear completely: its members were drafted into the commercial arm of the SED — the Socialist Unity Party. The SED set up a number of companies, moving into the west with haulage firms, trading operations in pharmaceuticals, timber, even soft toys. It was a wide network. It extended to Sierra Leone; it had representation in Beirut. But while its open activities were legitimate, Miss Witt believed that underneath lay more sinister acts. And Miss Witt believed that certain members of the death squad acted initially as enforcers, but later moved up into the commercial hierarchy. She was on their trail. Three men in particular. She named them in her files, apparently, so I was told by Hannah Guderian when she visited me here and asked for my assistance. Eigendorf, Vogel and Auerbach . . . all holding responsible positions in commercial companies but under assumed names, and all former members of the death squad.'

There was a short silence.

Jacobsen shifted in his wheelchair, easing his leg. 'If you are supporters of football, you will have heard of Dynamo Berlin.'

'So?' Eric asked.

'Did you know that it was actually a Stasi-backed football club?'

Eric frowned. 'Dieter Barschel—'

'He was a junior on the playing staff, until he moved on to Italy, and later England.' He sighed. 'I should never have divulged his location to Hannah Guderian . . .'

'But you've already said that Barschel would know nothing about the disappearance of Andrea Witt.'

Jacobsen shrugged. 'That is so. But I believe she saw him as another part of a jigsaw puzzle. If she could put all the pieces together, maybe she would discover the truth about the disappearance of her beloved half-sister.' He heaved a reluctant sigh. 'But these are dangerous matters to discuss. You will forgive me. I think that is all, gentlemen. These are not really matters in which I wish to become involved after so many years. I no longer possess the kind of zeal that led to the disappearance of Miss Witt. I live quietly; my pieces for the journals are uncontroversial. I only seek peace to live out my life.'

'You said you had copies of the articles Miss Witt wrote for the German newspapers,' Eric said. 'Can we take further copies?'

Jacobsen shook his head. 'No, you can take the originals. I no longer wish for involvement. I am too old. Since hearing about this accident to Hannah Guderian . . . I am sad. I wish I had not assisted her. But it was merely an oddment . . . I had followed the career of Dieter Barschel in football in the north-east. That was all I could tell her. That, and the fact that I suspected he had, in his early days with Dynamo Berlin, worked as an informant for the Stasi. But clearly, it was too much.'

He wheeled himself across the room, took from a cupboard a file of cuttings, and handed them to Eric. He followed them to the front door. 'I am sorry I could not help you more. But goodbye to you now, Mr Ward. And to your policeman friend.'

As they walked back along the street to the Tube station Charlie Spate growled, 'How the hell did he twig that I was a policeman?'

Eric grunted. 'Maybe his experiences of the past, in East Germany, are so deeply scored in his memory that he can't fail to recognise one when he sees one.'

Charlie wasn't happy. It was a disturbing thought that the old man should have regarded Charlie Spate in the same light as the dreaded Stasi secret police.

They hailed a cab near the Tube station. When they finally reached Heathrow they had an hour to wait before they caught the shuttle back to Newcastle. Eric pored over the cuttings provided by Jacobsen. His German was not good, but he managed to get the gist of what Andrea Witt had written both for *Bild and Tagesspiegel*. It mainly confirmed what Jacobsen had already told them. Spate wandered off, bought himself a pint of beer and came back to join Eric. 'Well, it's all a bit dramatic, hey? But somehow, it doesn't seem to gel with my view of life on Tyneside. In my experience, the villains along the river are just straightforward villains. Except for that bastard Vasagar.' He shook his head. 'But even him . . . I don't see him getting tangled up with the kind of people that came out of East Germany.'

'I agree,' Eric replied slowly. 'I think it's a bit of a red herring, but somehow or other we need to find out just what the hell Dieter Barschel was involved in.'

'It was certainly serious enough for someone to want to blow his head off,' Charlie Spate agreed, and took a long pull at his pint.

CHAPTER 10

It was an odd feeling, working so closely alongside Charlie Spate. On their return to Newcastle he and Eric had taken a meal together at a country pub, had discussed what they had learned, but agreed they were really no further forward. There was still a wariness in the relationship but at least they had a common aim in view. Before they parted Spate agreed to find out what he could about the progress of the investigation into the killing of Barschel, while Eric would make use of what contacts he had to discover what rumours were circulating along the river.

For Charlie Spate it meant seeking out Elaine Start; for Eric Ward a conversation with Jackie Parton was necessary.

When Charlie walked into Elaine Start's room at headquarters her reception of him was not welcoming. 'DCI Spate. What on earth are you doing here?'

Charlie grinned, and perched himself on the edge of her desk, one leg swinging. 'So they've given you a room to yourself instead of a desk in the main base of scene of crime room. Going up in the world, girl, aren't you?'

She gave him a sour glance, threw down her pen and leaned back in her chair. She took a deep breath. He enjoyed the manner in which her white shirt lifted and tightened.

'You're on suspension. You shouldn't be here. If the ACC comes across you—'

'Since when did Charteris walk beyond his office and the briefing room?' Charlie jeered. 'People go to him — he doesn't expect to have to spend time visiting the rabble at the coal face.'

She relaxed; now there was a hint of a smile on her mouth: Charlie liked her mouth, too. She shook her head. 'Even so, it was made clear you were to stay away from the station. What are you after anyway?'

He shrugged, reached out, turned the file on which she had been working to an angle where he could read its contents. She pulled it back away from him with a jerk. 'Just wanting to get up to speed, that's all,' he offered. 'Who knows, maybe the Chief will decide he can't do without my undoubted skills after all, and will beg me to come back, all forgiven. Now; it wouldn't do if I came back ignorant of what has been going on, would it?'

Elaine snorted in disbelief. 'Call you back? Pigs have a better chance of flying.'

'Nevertheless, why don't you tell me the present state of play? Can't do any harm.'

'DCI Spate, harm's your middle name.' Elaine hesitated, then sighed. 'Well, to begin with, I'm to be relieved of the investigation into Barschel's death. Charteris is drafting in Inspector Martin to take over: I'll be handing the files over to him end of the week.'

'So Joe Martin's in the chair. Solid enough guy,' Charlie admitted. 'But what have you found out so far?'

She grimaced. 'Not a great deal. The forensic report is in. It told us the cause of death, as though it wasn't obvious! The shotgun was clean — no prints, no information as to its provenance. Unusual to have the weapon left there like that at the crime scene — I don't know; but to me it suggests almost a kind of contempt. Anyway, we can't fix any trace on it other than a few fibre traces. Not much help, unless we find the killer wearing the actual jacket that matches the fibres! Barschel hadn't put up a fight, and there are suggestions from forensic that there was at least one other person at the cottage, apart from Barschel, his killer and Ward. Still no sign of a mobile phone. Barschel's personal belongings at the cottage were few; just stuffed in a holdall, personal things, and the suitcase mentioned by Eric Ward, well, still no sign of that. It looks as though all the killer or killers wanted was what was in the suitcase. They must have gone there to get it after he'd made a call. At least, that's what we're working on. At the moment, we're chasing up any acquaintances of the dead man that we can identify. But there were a hell of a lot of them — and mainly small shady characters on the edge of various villainy along the river.'

'While you've still been on the case, did you make any enquiries as to Barschel's background?' Charlie asked.

'How do you mean?' Elaine frowned.

'Well, you know, his early history.' Charlie said casually.

'He's been on Tyneside nearly twenty years. That's enough to get on with.' She paused, eyeing him carefully. 'Unless you know something we don't.'

For one tempting moment he was on the point of telling her about his visit to London, but he held back. The thought of Charteris had intervened. The ACC had suspended him; he had the shadow of an enquiry hanging over him; Charlie was not about to hand over information that might be important to him personally, if he was to get off the hook. He needed to come up with answers, both for himself and also to show that he wasn't the villain Charteris made him out to be. He shook his head. 'Not really. Just wondered, that's all. He was a Romanian and travelled a bit. Just a thought . . . maybe there'd be files on him.'

She watched him uncertainly for a few seconds, then shook her head. 'No, it's not a road I've gone down. And now it's Inspector Martin's pigeon, anyway.'

'I guess so. So what will you be concentrating on, DS Start?' She looked away. A certain evasiveness crept into her tone. 'You'll remember the ACC asked me to deal with liaison work — we're working with Cleveland Police, and now the Garda in Dublin as well.'

'Oho, trips to Old Oireland on the cards, hey,' he jeered. 'This in connection with the counterfeiting business, is that it? It'd be my guess the whole business, as far as we on the Tyne are concerned, could be settled by pulling in one man.'

'Now; I just wonder who that might be,' she replied sarcastically.

'Come on, you know as well as I do that Mark Vasagar will be behind it like he's behind most organised villainy along the river. A subtle and worthy successor to Mad Jack Tenby — who's playing golf with the Lord Lieutenant these days, I hear. Who says crime don't pay?'

Her gaze was stony. 'You should get rid of your obsessions, DCI Spate.'

He grinned. 'Not all of them, surely.'

He was rewarded by a slight flush in her cheek.

He stood up. 'Anyway, I'll be on my way if you've nothing else to report. But . . . er . . . one more thing. You say there were probably two people behind the shotgun at the cottage.'

Elaine Start nodded. 'So forensic would have us believe.'

'Both of them men?'

She widened her eyes. She regarded him with a hint of suspicion. 'Now you know that traditionally women are reputed to use much more feminine devices to kill — like poison. But why do you ask?'

So Eric Ward had ensured that there had been no traces left of the presence of Hannah Guderian at the cottage. Charlie Spate shook his head. 'No reason in particular.'

She eyed him steadily. 'All right. But I say it again — it's best you stay away from that enquiry. There's still a lot of rumours floating around about what you've been up to.'

'I bet there are,' he replied grimly.

'And keep your nose out of my assignment, sir. The counterfeiting. I . . . well, it's coming to a head. We've had a deal of information, and we think we'll be able to make a move soon. It's just a matter of checking a few sources in Dublin.'

Charlie Spate grinned broadly. 'And then you'll make your move against Mark Vasagar. I'd love to be around then, get sight of the arrogance knocked out of his supercilious face.'

For a moment he thought she was about to make an angry outburst at him, but she bit back the comment. He headed for the door. He stopped there for a moment, looked back at her. She was watching him, an odd expression in her eyes. Their glances locked.

'I'll tell you what, Charlie Spate,' she said softly. 'You've been a stupid bugger.'

Oddly enough the comment, and the look in her eyes, gave him scope for optimism.

* * *

Eric Ward also found scope for some optimism when he paid another visit to the hospital. He sought out the serious young doctor who was still in charge of Hannah Guderian.

'I'm glad to say there seems to be some considerable improvement, Mr Ward. Miss Guderian has come round, but she's still very weak, but the good thing is that the tests we've made on her nervous responses lead us to believe there has been no serious, irreparable damage. There's been no fracture of the skull; the pressure on the brain has been relieved. It's early to say, of course, and one can never be sure, but our prognosis, well, we've every hope that she'll make a good recovery in the next few days.'

It was good news and Eric went back to his office considerably relieved.

He had had a meeting with Jackie Parton and briefed him on what they had learned in London. Eric had felt a need to unburden himself. Jackie had listened without expression as Eric had outlined what had happened at the cottage but it was clear he thought that Eric had been sailing close to the wind. Still, it wasn't the first time. Eric had outlined what he wanted: the police would naturally be looking into Dieter Barschel's background, but they suffered from the disadvantages of officialdom. There were snitches to be found in the city but they were well known. They might talk to the police, but in most cases they were people who would be avoided, left on the periphery by those really in the know, and they would have little information to impart. Things were different with Jackie Parton. Eric had no doubt it was well enough understood that the ex-jockey worked hand in glove on occasions with Eric Ward, but a blind eye was cast to it. Jackie Parton was well known and liked, a local celebrity of a kind, and more importantly, he was trusted.

'What I need, Jackie, is whatever we can dig up, you know; local background on Barschel. I want to find out how he's been making a living these last few years. The story we got down in London explains why Hannah Guderian wanted to meet him, but that's stuff going back years, and I don't see it's relevant . . . there must be something buried in his recent activity that provides the reason why he was first set up, and then killed.'

Jackie cocked his head on one side, considered the matter. 'And this Guderian girl. You certain her running down wasn't just an accident?'

Eric had hesitated. 'I've thought a great deal about it. There's too much that's coincidental about it all. Barschel gets arrested on a trumped-up charge, with the connivance of . . . of a police officer.'

'Nothing new in that,' Jackie grunted contemptuously.

Eric ignored the comment. He felt it was not wise at this stage to mention the involvement of Charlie Spate, even though Jackie would have been aware of the remarks Eric had made in the Barschel preliminary hearing: after all, it was he who had provided Eric with the scuttlebutt along the river.

'I keep going over it in my mind. As soon as Barschel is released he wants me to find him a safe house. He has calls to make, he tells me. But it was clear that he was extremely angry about something, and intended getting revenge on whoever really set him up. Yes, the police were involved, but as far as I can make out there was someone in the shadows, someone who set up the whole thing. Romy Arendt might be able to give us a lead—'

Jackie shook his head doubtfully. 'I've asked around. The story is she's gone south. One source reckons she's left the country. Gone home.'

Eric considered the matter for a little while. 'That would mean either she was given a wad of money . . . or a warning.'

Jackie nodded. 'And the other guy, the nark who slipped the package into Barschel's pocket, he's not been around either, but I've got feelers out about him. There was some kind of deal going between him and Barschel but I'm not clear on it yet. Still, like the Arendt woman, he seems to have scarpered as well.' Jackie hesitated, grimaced thoughtfully. 'As far as I can make out, there's some heavy muscle around on this, Mr Ward.'

Eric nodded, shrugged, then suggested, 'There are some who believe Mark Vasagar is behind it; some play he's involved in.'

Jackie Parton screwed up his nose in a thoughtful grimace. 'I can't be sure about that. The whisper along the river is, well, he's reputed to be sort of snuggling up to the coppers recently. Hard to believe, but there it is. He's reckoned to have some kind of link, certainly, with someone among your former colleagues. Walking on the same bridge, like. But it's all a bit vague, and not many people want to talk about Mark Vasagar. You know how it is: you poke your nose in and the heavy muscle comes down on you. Then you wake up in a dark alley with your bones rearranged.' He managed a wry grin. 'I know that to my cost, from the old days. I still got aches and pains on damp days to remind me.'

Eric changed tack. 'What do you make of this thing Hannah Guderian was following up on?'

'East Germany? The Stasi death squad business?' Jackie shook his head in doubt. 'You tell me the German newspapers have been screaming about it these last few years, but it don't cut much ice up on the Tyne, Mr Ward. We got our own villains to worry about. But who knows? And the injuries on the girl up at Stanhope, well it could have been a simple hit and run. Some wild layabout in a car he's twocked, speedin' to show off to his girlfriend. That road in Stanhope, it's pretty narrow, there's a tempting straight stretch, and in the evening . . .'

'I don't know, Jackie.' Eric clucked his tongue in irritation. 'I still can't get it out of my mind. The car on the cliff: I'd assumed it was walkers up there, but it could have been someone who'd already been to the cottage, killed Barschel, and was hanging around to await events. Keeping an eye on the place. Then when we showed up, and I took Hannah to the hotel in Stanhope, it would have been easy enough to follow at a distance. Then, when she walked out to the phone box—'

'But why would they be after her, and not you?' Jackie asked. 'They'd have seen you both going into the cottage.'

'Because at that point I didn't know what she knew. And I still don't know all about it.'

Jackie Parton shook his head in doubt. 'It's streaky, Mr Ward.'

He knew it. 'Keep digging anyway, Jackie. See what you come up with. Then let me know as soon as you can.'

Meanwhile Eric had a living to earn. He called in each day during the following week to check on Hannah's progress and was informed she was in a stable condition but still unable to communicate. Vital life signs were good however, and she was out of her comatose condition. The rest of the time he was extremely busy. Media attention had been diverted by other events, as it inevitably was, and he was not bothered further by reporters apart from the odd inquisitive phone call, concerning the death of Dieter Barschel, and whether there had been further developments. There had been some speculation, of course, but most of the questions raised were directed at the police and the state of their investigation.

There had been two articles written in the local press about Barschel's brief career with Newcastle, and his subsequent appearances in the lower leagues, and two former players had cashed in with interviews describing the kind of man he was. But it was all ephemera, facile, shallow reporting and helped no one except the circulation managers for the newspapers.

Otherwise, for Eric there was an argument between two estate agents disputing a commission deal to be sorted out, and a drilling supply contract to be agreed with some ship brokers on the Tyne. He dealt with a group of disgruntled would-be tourists who were claiming their money back from a collapsed coach company. He obtained in his view a reasonable, but not to their minds, satisfactory settlement of their claims. He put pressure on an insurance company over a whiplash claim in a car accident, sorted out payments due under a hire purchase agreement, and spent a full day on a building site trying to arbitrate between an excavator driver who had caused an accident on site, the construction site manager, and the hirer of the earth-moving equipment. There were two county court appearances to make on behalf of clients arguing about a copyright issue, a wills dispute, and advice to give on protected tenancies in a block of flats near the Byker Wall where possession was sought by the landlord. It all became somewhat wearying, although he did manage a lunch with Sharon Owen, whom he was briefing on a marine insurance case.

'You're looking a bit harassed,' she suggested.

'I've got things on my mind,' he confessed.

'I read about your performance in front of Colonel Vaughan. In fact, there's been quite a bit of chat in our chambers about it. There's a general feeling you went a bit too far. My guess is, you were hoping for a result — but not in that courtroom.'

He smiled. He liked Sharon Owen; she was perceptive, beautiful and smart. 'It worked out in the end,' he admitted. 'The CPS decided to drop the charges.'

'Which is what you were hoping for. Not that it makes any difference now, with the man dead.' She observed him quietly, while he toyed with the seafood on his plate. 'You found his body, I understand. You know, if you want my advice, Eric, it would be better if you didn't get so . . . involved.'

She was right, of course. But at the moment he still held the vision of the girl in the hospital, still drifting, still unable to communicate properly.

'And talking of involvement,' Sharon remarked casually, 'I haven't seen much of you lately.' She paused, but when he made no reply, then added, 'How's Anne these days?'

He shrugged. 'I think she's getting over the business with Jason Sullivan. She's got plenty to do to take her mind off things.'

'While many of my evenings are lonely,' she commented archly.

He laughed it off. He was aware of the nascent feelings between them, but he was not prepared to commit to a relationship other than one based on friendship. She was an attractive woman, but he was not yet ready for commitment. It was nothing to do with his ex-wife: he believed now that their relationship had suffered too many painful emotional traumas. Yet perhaps it was because of that experience that he remained wary of involvement with Sharon Owen.

It was a thought that he was dwelling upon while he sat in his office in the early evening, watching the twinkling lights across the river, the Millennium Bridge and the Baltic Centre, and the reflective glazed roof of the newly erected Sage Centre. They were idle thoughts, really, a musing upon the past, the good years of his marriage to Anne, the tearing of the fabric of their relationship, and the suppressed rage behind his dealings with Jason Sullivan. The man seemed to have gone to ground now, somewhere in Europe: at least, he had left Anne's life. But there was still so much emotional scar tissue.

The telephone's shrill call dragged him back from his reverie. Susie and the legal executive had already left the office; he was alone. He picked up the phone.

'Mr Ward? I think we should meet.'

It was Jackie Parton. 'Have you come up with anything?'

'Can't be sure. But, well, you'd better talk to the man himself. You know McGillivray's Bar?'

'I think so. That place down at Shields?'

'That's the one. Tonight, if you can. Nine-thirty, say?'

'I'll be there.'

Eric replaced the phone and sat there for a while, thinking, unsure. At last he reached the decision: two heads were better than one. He called Charlie Spate.

'I think it would be a good idea if I picked you up at eight-thirty tonight.'

'This a social invitation?' Spate asked ironically.

'We'll be going out to Shields.'

CHAPTER 11

No one knew why he was called Calico Jim, and he professed to have forgotten the reason himself.

He wore a misshapen, battered dungaree cap on his shaven skull and his skin had a corrugated appearance, lined by wind and weather. Grey stubble covered the lower half of his face and his teeth were yellow; nicotine stained. He wore a discoloured reefer jacket summer and winter and a red neckerchief that he claimed had once belonged to Lloyd George. The boast was so absurd that no one ever bothered challenging it.

In earlier years he had told tall tales about rounding the Horn in a sailing ship but he could not have been much more than seventy years of age and the general opinion was that he had never sailed further south than Redcar and further north than Amble, and even that was doubtful. The parentage he claimed was bastard, from the Dacre family, but since he had difficulty even spelling the name that also was deemed false. Men of his generation said he had turned up on Tyneside some forty years ago, a layabout from Liverpool, but if so he had lost all trace of a Scouse accent and was now reckoned to be a Geordie by adoption if not by birth. He seemed to spend most of his days scrounging around in the bins at

North Shields; he occasionally appeared at Seahouses though he never divulged how he got there, and he frequented five different pubs in the Shields area. He always carried a pocketful of change, though he had become such an institution in the taverns that he could always find one or two people to buy him a drink. He tended to nurse his drinks, and had never been seen drunk. But he was always garrulous.

When Eric walked into the snug at McGillivray's Bar he caught sight of him immediately, seated in the corner with Jackie Parton. Jackie raised his head and began to rise but when he caught sight of the man entering the bar behind Eric the welcoming glint in his eyes faded. Eric walked up to the bar and ordered drinks for himself and Charlie Spate; the policeman took the opportunity to wander away for a few minutes to watch a raucous darts match in the public bar beyond the snug.

Jackie Parton was swiftly at Eric's elbow.

'What'll you have to drink, Jackie?' Eric asked, knowing what was coming.

'A pint for each of us will do: Newcastle Brown for the old man.' He leaned closer to Eric. 'What the hell you doin' bringin' that man here? I was expecting you by yerself, Mr Ward, and now you turn up with one of the fuzz! What's going down, man?'

'DCI Spate has been suspended, as you'll have heard. I didn't tell you earlier, but he went down to London with me. We've both got a personal interest in what's going on. We're working together, and I think we can help each other.' The drinks were placed on the bar in front of him. 'Trust me on this one, Jackie.'

The ex-jockey was unhappy and made his feelings plain. 'Don't know about this, Mr Ward. I don't like dealing direct with the polis.' He glanced over Eric's shoulder; Spate was sauntering back from the darts match. 'Looks like I don't have much choice in the matter though, doesn't it?'

Sourly, he picked up the two pints and slouched his way back to the corner seats. Charlie Spate looked at Eric, raised his eyebrows; he could guess exactly what was going on. He followed Eric across the snug, to take seats beside Jackie and Calico Jim. Reluctantly, Jackie said, 'These are two friends of mine, Jim.'

'Any friend of Jackie,' wheezed the old man, 'can be regarded as a friend of mine.' Even so, his eyes rested on Eric for a while, weighing him up. 'Seen you around. Didn't you use to be a copper, way back?'

'More than a few years ago,' Eric admitted.

'Thought I seed you. Got a good memory has Calico Jim.' He sipped noisily at his ale. He then turned his head, looked at Charlie Spate; there was a shade of suspicion in his heavily pouched eyes, but he said nothing, and made no suggestion that Charlie should be introduced to him. Eric was certain that the old man would recognise Spate if he came across him again; he was equally sure that Calico Jim had guessed Spate was a police officer. He just hoped that the knowledge would not make him close up like an oyster.

'Calico Jim's been telling me about the old days along the river,' Jackie muttered unhappily, still resenting the presence of Charlie Spate.

'Oh, and how was it?' Spate asked in a cheerful tone. 'Full of bonny lads and lasses, hey?'

'I can tell you're not from around here or you wouldn't talk so daft,' the old man snorted scornfully. 'Life was bloody hard, ye knaa, down in the dockyards and down in the pits.' He shrugged, then chuckled malignantly. 'Not that I never did a day's work in either of them.'

'It's a mystery what the hell you ever did,' Jackie Parton commented, relaxing somewhat, though when he glanced at Eric there was still a shadow of resentment in his eyes. 'Or for that matter, what keeps you in one piece these days.'

'Ahah! I do a bit of this and a bit of that. But it's a long time,' he leered, 'since I seen a bit of the other! Not that I wasn't a canny lad with the lasses when I was young. Though I always preferred them a bit on the big side, nothing scrawny for me. Something to hang on to when you're at it, you know what I mean?'

'Being always around, though,' Eric suggested carefully, 'you manage to see what's going on, and who's up to what?'

'You can say that again,' Calico Jim boasted, 'and keep on sayin' it. There's not much happens along the river that I don't know of. Me and Jackie, we're like little rats scurrying along on the banks, noses twitching, eyes agleam. In that right, Jackie?'

The ex-jockey clearly felt unflattered by the description. But he managed a grin. 'Well, I'd have put it a different way. But that's right, we get to know more or less what's happening around Newcastle, Shields and Byker.'

Calico Jim sipped again at his pint, smacked his lips in appreciation. He leaned back on the settle and scratched at his stubbly beard. He took a long look at Eric. 'Jackie was tellin' me how you was defendin' Dieter Barschel the other day, and stuffed one to the polis.'

Charlie Spate wriggled a little on his chair, but said nothing. 'Like to see a man do that from time to time,' Calico Jim offered, making a purring sound deep in his old throat. 'Not that I don't have a good relationship with them coppers personally, from Seahouses to Shields.' His careful eyes slid towards Spate, and he smiled conspiratorially. 'Always does good to keep well in with the polis, is my motto.'

'So did you know Dieter Barschel well?' Eric asked, changing the subject as he became uncomfortably aware of Charlie Spate's unease.

His casual tone did not fool the old man, but it was clear he had already been briefed by Jackie Parton. 'Dieter Barschel? Aye, well enough. Not in his glory days when he had money to spend and was free with it they say. I was never one of the Toon Army, yer see, not one of those ravin' lunatics who support Newcastle and then beat up the town on a Saturday night after that match. Naa, I got to know him later, when he was on the skids, like. They say it was the drink after he got his legs broke and frittered away a couple of years in the Durham League, but I reckon it was more like the drugs, cos they was usin' them in those days, like and don't let anyone tell you to the contrary.'

'Did he ever talk to you about his background, his early days before he came to England?'

Calico Jim wrinkled his veined nose. 'Him? Can't say so. I heerd from other folk that he was a pretty good footballer in his day and he was a furriner, like, wasn't he? They breed them, you knaa, footballers. They got these camps that wos set up by Adolf in the old days and they chose these kids and they drilled 'em, and it's nivver been a fair fight. Not the way we ever worked in this country. No surprise we only won the World Cup once, and they say that was a fix. Wouldn't surprise me.'

Eric caught a glint of amusement in Jackie Parton's eyes. It was not going to be easy to keep Calico Jim to the point.

'I think you're confusing the Hitler Youth with the East German regime after the war,' Eric suggested with a smile. 'But did he ever tell you about what life was like in East Germany?' Calico Jim frowned, pursed his lips. 'I allus thought Dieter Barschel was a Romanian. That's what he told me, anyways. I remember the occasion. We was—'

'Yes, he was Romanian,' Eric interrupted hastily, 'but he played football for Dynamo Berlin, before moving on to Italy.'

'Now is that a fact?' Calico Jim said in a tone lacking in interest. He liked to talk, not listen.

'So he never talked about those days?'

'No. I suppose you knew about it because you was his lawyer. What was the name of the copper you stiffed when you was acting for Barschel the other week?'

'It's no matter,' Jackie Parton intervened quickly as he saw Charlie Spate beginning to bridle. 'Never mind about that. If there's nothing you can tell Mr Ward about Barschel in the old days—'

'Nivver talked much about that,' the old man admitted.

'How did he make a living recently?' Eric asked. 'I mean, was it anything to do with the racetrack?'

Calico Jim screwed up his face, leaned forward and regarded with interest the dilapidated Adidas trainers that he wore on his grimy, sockless feet. 'Got those out of a bin in Byker. Kids these days . . . throwaway really good stuff. Just as well for me, mind. Barschel was a bit like me in that respect. He rooted around a bit, got a shift here, a scam there. But more recently, he was working as a runner.'

Charlie Spate leaned forward. 'What do you mean, a runner? Taking bets for the bookies?'

Calico Jim guffawed. 'Haway, man. You're talkin' through yer arse! Them days is long gone. I used to work as a bookie's runner meself, but that was years since, when I was but a kid in Liverpool. Hey, I used to work for a bookie then, collectin' bets when it was against the law to do any bettin' off course. Only at the racetrack itself, you could do, or by post, of course. Me, I used to wait outside the cathedral in Liverpool till the congregation came out, and after they'd been to mass, why you wouldn't believe how eager they were for a bet. Mind you, I've always said, them Roman Catholics is buggers for a bet and the Irish worst of all! They was only beaten in their enthusiasm by those Chinese: now they're really addicted to the gambling. Why I seen them in their temples, with the joss sticks waving, prayin' to their heathen gods with a racing paper spread out in front of them. Now if that ain't an addiction I don't knaa what is!'

'Chinese temple? You never saw any such thing,' Jackie scoffed. 'You never sailed further than the mouth of the Tyne.'

The old man displayed yellow teeth, unoffended. 'Well, I must've seen it in some magazine, then. But Catholics, don't talk to me about them. I lost that little job in Liverpool when the guy who used to collect the tithes for the Church took up the sideline of collecting the bets. Hell, it was immoral, I tell you!'

Patiently, Eric asked, 'But Dieter Barschel wasn't taking bets on the racecourse. Was he working as some kind of runner for the bookmakers?'

'Na, na, na, you got it all wrong,' Calico Jim chided. 'He'd been working for months for that cocky bastard Toddy

Cleaver. I can tell you about him. Cleaver's always been a nasty piece of work. I'm not one to talk too much, and I don't nail people even if I don't like them.' Suddenly, there was real venom in the old man's voice, and Eric began to understand why Jackie Parton had persuaded Calico Jim to talk. 'Toddy Cleaver was always a tearaway. I had thirty years on him of course, but that made no difference. If I had been younger he'd have ended up in hospital that night. The bastard took offence at some story I was telling — he was drunk, mind, I'll say that in all fairness but it don't matter — and he come across the pub and he dragged me out by the scruff and he gave me a right kickin'. Broke a couple of my ribs, he did, but that wasn't all. That night, he wos drunk so, OK, maybe I had something coming, me and my big mouth. It's what happened next, that was the clincher fer me.'

He picked up his pint, studied it malevolently for a moment and then sipped at it, deep in reflection.

'He and his mates, they found me down at the Black Rocks two nights later. I was mindin' my own business, you understand, pickin' up a few clams on the beach there. They hadn't been drinking much that evening, well, not much anyway. You know what they did? They threw some lighter fuel at me, and then when me rags was drippin', like, they kept throwin' matches at me. In the end I went up like a bloody Roman candle . . .'

There was silence suddenly around the table. Eric glanced at Charlie Spate. His mouth was set hard, his eyes expressionless.

'Course, I did a straight jig off the rocks into the sea. But I got some bad burns. That Toddy Cleaver. I always said he was a mad bugger, and I'd get him some dark night for those burns . . . I was three days in the General Infirmary gettin' treatment. But somehow, I never got the chance, or I suppose never had the muscle to get back at him.'

'Till now, maybe,' Charlie Spate suggested quietly.

The old man's eyes gleamed as he stared at Spate; there was agreement in the glance.

'You were saying Dieter Barschel was working as a runner for this man Toddy Cleaver,' Eric prompted. 'I still don't understand. You mean he was linking up with the bookies—'

Calico Jim shook his head despairingly. 'Come on, don't you know the score? Yeah, Barschel was working for Toddy Cleaver, and he had links with three of four of the on-course bookies, but he wasn't taking bets! He was playing with funny money.'

Eric was aware of a sudden tension in the man seated beside him. 'Funny money?' Charlie Spate repeated. 'You mean counterfeit notes?'

Calico Jim regarded him with a certain contempt. 'Well, aye, man. That's what I said. Funny money. It's been going on a while. The lads are being very careful these days. They take a bloody good look at whatever they're picking up on the side. It's been coming in from Cleveland, the story goes . . . You see, this is why Toddy Cleaver will never make it as big as he thinks he will. He makes out he's a smart operator, but he's really just a thick thug who's got too big for his boots. He might employ muscle, he might have set up this organisation, he might be using contacts on the racecourse to spread the money around, but he's got a big mouth. If it wasn't for his partner, the Irishman—'

'Wait a minute,' Eric interrupted. He hesitated as a roar went up in the bar, where the darts match was just ending. 'You're saying Barschel was helping move counterfeit money around the track. When he was arrested—'

Calico Jim grunted contemptuously. 'That was another seam. The polis got involved there, the hell knows why. But it was all a set-up.' The old man shook his head. 'Dieter Barschel was expecting a drop into his pocket. The system was that the money got shuffled around between bookies and punters, it was his job to take a few packets from the grifters, and move it on by placing a bet — not a real one, of course — and then repeat the procedure. But when he got this particular drop, he realised it wasn't right somehow. I don't know, the story is maybe it was the wrong weight, wrong shape or whatever, but he got wind of trouble so he decided to leg it. But the polis, they knew all about it. They nailed him. Drugs! Come on, Barschel never did drugs! He might have used them years ago, but he was no dealer and this, hey, it was a polis plant!'

There was an awkward, strained silence. 'What?' snapped the old man, glaring around. 'You don't believe me?'

Eric glanced at Charlie Spate. The man's face was grim. Jackie Parton shuffled in his seat. 'Was Toddy Cleaver involved in this somehow?'

'If he was working for the coppers. But I wouldn't know. I don't think that bastard would sink that low.'

Eric was about to speak when Charlie Spate grated, 'A counterfeit notes scam. This character Toddy Cleaver ran it, but you said—' He broke off for a moment as a cheer went up from the bar, and then there was the sound of a fiddle starting up in a mad jig. Calico Jim clapped his hands. 'That's what I like about this place. A few nights a week, the Irish bastards go wild with the jigs! They're mostly Geordies, of course, but they still reckon they got close emotional links to the Old Country.'

Charlie Spate was undeterred. Above the wild screeching of the fiddle he said, 'You mentioned an Irishman, involved with Cleaver.'

'That's so, that's so.' Incredibly, the sound of the fiddle, joined now by a second one, made Calico Jim adopt an Irish accent.

'You know his name?'

'Hell, I don't know. I might have heard him called Seamus somewhere or other. But nothing more than that. He sometimes comes into McGillivray's when the fiddlers are in. So can we now enjoy the music? Ah, 'tis a great sound, the fiddle, to be sure.'

Amazed and amused by the false Irish accent, Eric leaned back in his chair, watching Calico Jim beat out the rhythm on the table in front of him. Charlie Spate scraped back his chair as he stood up. He took his drink and walked across to the doorway of the snug to observe the fiddlers and the men banging glasses to the rattling, screeching noise. After a while Eric rose and joined him. Spate was silent, head lowered, occasionally sipping his drink, watching the faces of the men crowded around the bar. His shoulder was touching Eric's; suddenly Eric felt it tense. 'What's the matter?' Eric asked.

Charlie Spate hesitated, then turned away. 'Nothing. I've had enough. You think the old man has anything else to tell us?'

'I'm not sure. If he has, Jackie will be able to let me know.'

'I've had enough. Let's be off.' He began to drain his glass. Jackie Parton was making his way towards them. He stood in front of Charlie Spate, glowering, waited until the drink was finished. 'You'll understand, Mr Spate, this is a one-off. I don't like working directly with the polis.'

'Understood, Mr Parton.' Charlie Spate dug in his back pocket, pulled out his wallet, drew out a twenty-pound note. He offered it to the ex-jockey. 'Give this to Calico Jim.'

Jackie stared at the offering. He did not reach out to take it. 'He won't welcome it, Mr Spate.'

Spate's glance hardened. 'Give it to him. He's been useful. He's not far from the gutter. He could use the money. Damn it, Parton, I feel sorry for him!'

Woodenly, Jackie Parton said, 'He doesn't take money, Mr Spate, only favours from his friends. I'll look after him. Put your money away.'

Charlie Spate glared at him, then shrugged, turned away and headed for the door. After he had gone, Eric said, 'I brought him here. I'll have to give him a lift back. Jackie—'

There was hurt in Jackie Parton's eyes. 'Like I said to Mr Spate, this has got to be a one-off, Mr Ward. I don't like dealing with the polis.'

He turned away and re-joined the old man in the corner. As he left Eric was very conscious of the rheumy eyes of Calico Jim fixed on his retreating back.

CHAPTER 12

The tunes the fiddle played stayed in Charlie Spate's head all night, until he finally fell asleep in the early hours of the morning, and they returned as soon as he awoke. But it was not simply the tunes: they formed the background sound to a face.

Charlie Spate was pretty good with faces; the problem was he often had difficulty putting a name to a face. While Eric Ward had still been at the corner table with Calico Jim and Jackie Parton, Charlie had stood at the doorway to the bar area, watching proceedings. At that point there had been two fiddlers sawing away frenetically and yet in complete control; they were in the centre of the room, in front of the dartboard, and a space had been cleared for them. At the bar, and in a group facing the fiddlers, there were about a dozen men, some young, others perhaps in their forties, but despite the discrepancy in ages their enthusiasm was mutual. They were laughing, singing, clapping their hands to the beat and thoroughly enjoying themselves.

Charlie could see some of the faces in profile, but other men had their backs to him. He scanned the faces carefully, but there was no one he recognised, not that he had really expected to: he had never been in McGillivray's Bar before and he suspected that these men would probably be regular visitors. He was about to turn away and go back to join the others when one of the men whose back he could see turned his head, and called out to the barman for a round of drinks. Charlie stared at him, a vague shadow of memory flitting through his mind. He was aware that Eric Ward had joined him, but his gaze remained fixed on the dark, stubble-haired man at the back of the group. Drinks were being lined up and the man moved away from the handclapping group to pick up a couple of pint glasses. As he turned, the man's eyes caught Charlie's and he grinned to see the two men in the doorway, apparently drawn by the fiddlers. There was no recognition in his eyes when he glanced at Charlie, but the shadow fluttered again as Charlie saw the man's full face.

The solicitor's shoulder was touching his and some-thing must have been communicated to him. Ward asked him what the matter was, but Charlie shook his head. He was disturbed; the stubble-haired man was someone he should know: But the elusive shadow in his mind danced and flut-tered away as the fiddlers screeched their tunes and men stood clapping and laughing and singing.

It was the same in the morning: the tunes in his head, the glimpse of a man's face.

He tried to clear them away, removing the clutter that prevented him concentrating on what they had learned from Calico Jim the previous evening. Irritably, he decided he would call in at Ward's office again: they had both been silent in the car after leaving McGillivray's Bar, each keeping his own thoughts to himself. Charlie rang Ward's office, to be told that the solicitor had gone to the hospital. Charlie decided to do the same: he had yet to see the mysterious Miss Hannah Guderian.

When he arrived at the hospital and produced his iden-tity warrant card he was allowed through to the ward where the girl was being kept, but was advised he would not be able to interview her. 'Miss Guderian's solicitor is with her at the moment, on condition he doesn't overtax her.'

'She's out of her coma?' Charlie asked.

'Absolutely. But she's in a weak state, and confused.' Charlie made his way to the ward door. Through the window he could see Eric Ward, standing beside the girl's bedside. Ward was holding her hand; the young woman seemed to be half asleep, perhaps drifting in and out of consciousness. There was a nurse standing to one side. As he watched, Ward said something to the nurse, who nodded, and Ward released the girl's hand, laid it gently on the sheet that covered her. He turned, saw Charlie at the door and came out of the room.

'I'm surprised to see you here.'

Charlie nodded to the silent figure in the bed. 'Thought I'd come around to see her, find out how she's getting on, having heard so much about her these last few days.'

'She's coming through, but she can't really talk very much,' Ward advised. 'And I doubt that she's got much memory of the events up at the cottage and Stanhope anyway.'

'Well, maybe it will all come back . . . I really wanted to have a word with you,' Charlie admitted.

'About last night? Let's get a coffee.' The solicitor led the way along the hospital corridors to the coffee shop located just inside the main entrance. Charlie took a seat at one of the tables while Ward bought two coffees. A man on the next table was reading a newspaper with one eye; the other was heavily bandaged. Further along was a man on crutches. Charlie didn't like hospitals: too many walking wounded. The solicitor joined him, carrying two plastic cups. 'They don't extend to decent cups in this place. Don't burn your fingers.'

'I've already had my fingers burned,' Charlie admitted sourly.

Eric Ward glanced at his companion. 'The girl, you mean?'

Charlie nodded. 'Romy Arendt. I get the feeling from what Calico Jim told us last night, that I was set up as much as Dieter Barschel. It's all getting clear: she was paid to give me the lead on Barschel, persuade me to help her — telling me Barschel was bothering her after their previous relationship had broken down — and I fell for it. To me, it was a matter of keeping a woman happy, and getting a drugs bust at the same time. An easy ride. I was stupid.'

Eric Ward made no comment. In the past, he had made a similar mistake himself, getting involved with the wrong kind of woman.

'And in spite of what Calico Jim told us, it now looks to me as though Toddy Cleaver might have been behind it. Calico Jim thinks not; me, I've got a different slant on it. But if Cleaver did put Romy Arendt up to it, what was in it for him? Why would he pay Romy Arendt to get me to stick the police onto Barschel? Was there bad blood between Cleaver and Barschel? There's something missing in all this. I just wondered whether you had any ideas.'

Eric Ward shrugged, picked up his plastic cup carefully and sipped at the hot coffee. He grimaced. 'Like you, I'm still puzzled. There's no obvious link to connect Cleaver with the framing of Barschel, and again, there's no reason I can perceive at the moment why Cleaver should have had anything to do with Barschel's death. I've been going around in circles with it all night—'

'Talk to me about it,' Spate grumbled.

'All I can think is that maybe the counterfeiting business is just background noise, confusing us. I can't see any reason why Dieter Barschel was killed, unless it was because Hannah Guderian arrived on the scene.'

'No, hold on there. Hannah Guderian popped up only *after* Barschel got arrested,' Charlie reasoned. 'She couldn't have been the trigger in all this.' He shook his head mournfully. 'All we do have is that Barschel worked for Cleaver, that he was a runner at the track, he was arrested in a put-up job, and after he got bailed he got stiffed, while Hannah Guderian almost got the same. But where's the connection? What's the reason behind it?'

Eric Ward frowned. 'I've puzzled over it. So much so I rang Jackie Parton this morning. He was able to give me an address.'

'Toddy Cleaver?' Spate guessed.

Eric nodded. 'He's got a place in Benton. Detached house on a small estate.' He eyed Charlie Spate warily. 'You think we should take a look?'

'I'm suspended,' Charlie grunted. 'Hey, I got nothing else to do.'

They took Eric Ward's Celica. They drove through the city suburbs towards Benton. Ominous clouds had piled up in the west and a drizzle of rain appeared on the windscreen. When they reached the estate where Cleaver's house was situated they slowed. Eric Ward turned left into the avenue. There were several cars parked in the roadway; they drove slowly past them. One was a dilapidated-looking Ford. Eric Ward peered through the windscreen. 'I think that'll be the house over—'

'Keep going,' Charlie ordered suddenly. 'Pick up speed and get out of this road.'

Startled, Eric glanced at the policeman but did as he was instructed. They swung around the corner, and when Spate turned his head to look back into the avenue Eric pulled in at the kerb. 'What was that about?'

Charlie Spate grimaced. 'Did you see that car, the battered-looking Ford? It's got a better engine than you might imagine. Souped-up, in fact.'

'What the hell are you talking about?' Eric asked, irritated.

'I know that car. I've used it myself. I know the registration number by heart.'

'I still don't know—'

'It's a bloody *police* car. Our friend Toddy Cleaver is under police surveillance!'

* * *

After Eric Ward dropped Charlie back at the hospital car park so he could recover his own vehicle, Charlie stayed in the car park for a while, while the solicitor drove away. He had things to think about. The jigsaw was getting complicated: he needed to clear away some clutter. At last he made up his mind, started the car and drove back into the city.

He arrived at headquarters and made his way up the stairs to the corridor that led to Elaine Start's room. Half way up the stairs he came face to face with ACC Charteris. The man stopped, glowered at him. 'Spate. You're on suspension. What the hell are you doing here?'

Charlie managed an air of injured innocence. 'Just some personal things in my desk, sir. Dropped by to pick them up.'

Charteris hesitated, frowned. 'Well make sure you get off the premises in double quick time. Stay away, you understand? I don't want you interfering in the Barschel enquiry — that's Inspector Martin's pigeon now. And there's nothing else of interest here to drag you in now. You'll be hearing from us early next week: you'll be called to present yourself in the Chief's office where some preliminary questions will be asked about what the hell you've been up to.'

'I'll be ready, sir.' Charlie's tone was almost humble.

Elaine Start was in her room. She was standing at her desk, a bundle of files in her arms. She was clearly about to leave to attend a meeting. She groaned audibly when she saw him. 'DCI Spate. Have you got no sense? If the ACC sees you—'

'Already crossed his path. Like you warned me, he wasn't pleased. But I can see you're on your way out, so this is just a quick visit. Can I give you a name?'

She glared at him suspiciously. 'What name?'

'Toddy Cleaver.'

There was a long, strained silence. At last she grunted, stared at him angrily. Slowly, she replaced the files on the desk in front of her. She took a deep breath. 'Where did you get that name?'

'He's under surveillance, isn't he?'

Elaine Start shook her head. 'Look, I'm not at liberty to—'

'He's your case. You're keeping an eye on him because you know he's tied in with this counterfeit notes business.'

She hesitated, glanced at her watch, then sat down. 'How the hell did you know that? Only the team—'

'Never mind that. What's the full story? No need to hold out on me, I've got bits of it anyway. Cleaver. The race-track. Distributing counterfeit notes. I'll give you something else. Did you know Dieter Barschel was a runner for Cleaver, working with some bent bookies in front of the stands?'

She grimaced. Hesitantly, she asked, 'Are you sure of that? We're treating them as two separate investigations! Barschel's killing is one thing, Cleaver's counterfeit distribution is another. It's not come to our attention that Barschel and Cleaver were connected. How did you come by this information?'

'Contacts, love. Like all DCIs have. So what have you got? I'll keep it to myself. I'm suspended, remember.'

She was far from happy. She thought about it for a while, then she shrugged. 'I suppose you can have it. Now you know what we're up to you might as well have what we've got.' She planted her hands on the desk in front of her, stared at them unhappily. 'According to the Cleveland police, a couple of years ago counterfeit notes started appearing in the area. Cleveland put a team onto it, and later, when the distribution became wider, they called us in.'

'The funny money was being shifted at the racetrack at Gosforth.'

Elaine Start nodded. 'As it had been in York previously. There are other distribution centres, apparently: Newcastle was the latest to come into the system.'

'Where's the money coming from?' Charlie asked.

'Ireland. It was the Cleveland police who made the breakthrough as regards the location of the printing firm. That's why they involved the Garda. It seems there's two brothers by the name of Flaherty in a Dublin back street.

They run a legitimate printing business, but some time ago they were joined by a designer by the name of Gilligan, one of those nerdish computer experts, a youngster, but skilled, you know what I mean? We still don't know how much he was taught, or by whom, or how he picked up the skills he does have, but anyway, we know that he is responsible for the design of the notes. And I tell you, they're damned good!'

'So the notes are produced in Dublin,' Charlie mused. 'Sterling only?'

'Seems so,' Elaine nodded. 'We've been in touch with Europol, who've got their own problems with counterfeit euro notes, but that's an ongoing thing. No, it seems the brothers Flaherty and their little designer Mr Gilligan are contenting themselves at the moment with an attempt to inflate, in their own little way, the British economy with their nasty little wares.'

'So when do you move in?' Charlie queried.

Elaine Start hesitated. 'Now look, DCI Spate, this is still under wraps. We've got to coordinate things with the Garda, of course. But our intelligence suggests there will be a new shipment of notes coming in soon, probably next week. As soon as we get information that it's arriving, and the local shipment for the Tyne takes place, the Garda will make the bust at the Flaherty printing works, Cleveland will sort out their end, and we'll move in on the distribution network here, in Newcastle.'

'And that means Toddy Cleaver?'

She took a deep breath and nodded. 'That's right. As far as we can make out, he's running the distribution at the racetrack and elsewhere. Now have you got what you want? Will you get out from under my feet?'

'DS Start, you are a most efficient police officer. I look forward with great anticipation to working with you again.'

'If you ever get the chance, the way you're going on!'

He raised a hand. 'Don't worry about it. Be optimistic, like me. One more thing. You got any other names, other than Toddy Cleaver?'

She shook her head. 'There'll be others, but it looks as though he's running the distribution system as his own show.' She glared at him. 'Mark Vasagar is not involved, whatever you may think!'

'Ah, it'll take a lot to convince me of that!' Charlie insisted.

'Dammit, you're so bloody wrong!' She was exasperated; it caused her to be indiscreet. 'The fact is, Mark Vasagar has been *helping* us on this!' He could see immediately that she regretted telling him. She picked up the files, and barged past him angrily. 'Now get off your hobbyhorse, DCI, get back home and put on your slippers, grab a pipe if you have to, stare at the ceiling and blow smoke rings! There's some of us got work to do!'

* * *

DCI Spate, suspended or not, had no intention of putting on his slippers and resting his feet. There were still fiddle tunes in his head and an image of a man's face. So, instead of taking Elaine Start's advice, he made his way to the left wing of the building and the records room. The officer in charge, Sergeant James, was nearing retirement, but was known for his truculent ways. His truculence was largely directed towards the top brass, however, it partly derived from the fact he felt he had several times been passed over for promotion, and had been sidetracked into a boring job.

When Charlie walked into the records room James swivelled in his chair and regarded him dispassionately. 'Well, well, well, DCI Spate. I'm surprised to see you. I heard you'd been suspended.'

'So many people have told me that I'm beginning to believe it,' Charlie replied sourly.

'So you want to look up your personal file here, see what smut they got on your record card, is that it?'

'Hell, I don't need to look it up. I know what I've been up to up here, and at the Met as well. No doubt there'll be stuff on file about my years there, and all my wayward wrongdoing.'

'I wouldn't know,' James replied fingering his double chin thoughtfully. 'Of course, I heard some chat about your cowboy methods down there, but personal files are under lock and key. I don't spend my spare time reading them. I mean, if I started, where would I stop? So, you just come here for a chat, or are you looking for something particular?'

Charlie knew the right buttons to press. 'Something that would explain why I've been set up would be nice.'

James's grizzled head came up and his eyes glittered. 'Set up, hey? And just who would be trying to set up a senior officer like a DCI?'

'Only someone more senior, like an Assistant Chief Constable.'

He'd struck the right note. James's mouth twisted. 'I can guess. Jim Charteris. So he's sticking in the knife, is he?' His body language suddenly expressed cooperation. 'So what specifically are you looking for?'

'Europol files.'

'That's easy enough. We got a stack of them. They're computerised of course. There's a PC over there you can set up, and I can give you the files. But there's a lot of them. Could be a long haul for you.'

Charlie thought for a while, then said, 'It'll be in with the stuff that came out of the Home Office, via Europol. Enquiries about individuals . . . as far as I recall they include mug shots.'

'So you want to trawl through the pretty boy picture album? Good luck, DCI Spate. It'll take you a while. Where do you want to start? We got villains from Spain, Portugal, France and Ethiopia; there's uglies from Jamaica, Nigeria and Germany; if you want to start alphabetically, there's Antigua — we had quite a few recently, Home Office queries on black gangs in London, and Europol information on their movements.'

At McGillivray's Bar, Calico Jim had mentioned the name *Seamus*.

'Let's try Ireland.'

Sergeant James stood up, leaned on one of the shelves stacked with files from years earlier. 'That's a whole world in itself, Mr Spate.'

Charlie thought about his time in the Met. Towards the end, there had been an enquiry, and something nagged at his mind, the dancing, fading image that had been conjured up when he had seen the man in McGillivray's Bar. 'The Derry killings,' he said.

The records officer raised his eyebrows. 'Now you're talking. But they were thirty years ago.'

'No, I'm interested in more recent enquiries.'

James nodded. 'Ah, the peace agreement, and all matters pertinent. In 1998 I remember we got quite a bit of stuff in from the Home Office about that. Some of the ballistics advisers were arguing it would be possible to establish whether any of the rifles used by the Army in the Bloody Sunday killings had been altered by insertion of a .22 calibre sleeve inside the barrel.'

Charlie nodded. 'I remember. The lawyers for the nationalists were claiming that the altering of the rifles would support their claim that paratroopers had been sent to Derry with specific orders to open fire on the rioters. They wanted access to the rifles so they could do their own checking. To make sure there was no cover-up.'

'That's right. The sleeve would allow marksmen to hit known troublemakers with precision, so as to avoid what they called collateral damage to bystanders.' James chuckled cynically and scratched his grizzled head. 'Wonderful the phrases these Army characters come up with to avoid telling the plain truth. Collateral damage . . . when they meant *killing innocent bystanders*.'

'I'd like to see the 1998 files. I seem to remember there were a number of individuals identified, as being sought for evidential purposes.'

'I'll see what I can find.'

He vanished towards the back of the room, behind some shelving, and Charlie heard boxes being moved around. After a few minutes the records officer returned, carrying three floppy disks. He handed them to Charlie and gestured to the PC he had referred to. 'Good luck. Hope you find what you want. And I hope when you find it, it'll help screw some bastard up above. They screwed enough of the rest of us, over the years.'

Charlie sat in front of the PC, switched on, inserted the first disk. He trawled through the index, opened a few files, but found nothing of interest. The problem was his memory was fuzzy, he was uncertain about precisely what he was looking for.

All he felt was that when it turned up, if it turned up, he'd know immediately. A face on a file.

He switched to the second disk. It looked more promising.

There was a list of Europol responses to Home Office requests that had then been circulated to the provincial forces. One of them was headed *Contempt and Resistance*. He clicked on the file.

Persistent obstruction has been noted from staff at the Dolphin Street legal offices in answering and dealing with requests for information regarding the provision of an audit trail to connect serial numbers of pistols recovered from the scene at Derry with offences committed on January 30, 1972. Since the disbandment of the legal office at Dolphin Street, several of the staff have disappeared. Efforts should be made to trace these men, who it is suspected have joined friends and supporters in England. Three men in particular are believed to have been working at Dolphin Street undercover, and are believed to have been involved in several bank robberies in the north. Details appended.

There were photographs of three men. The second of them immediately caught Charlie's attention. The hair was longer; the thin face less lined. But he had no doubt. It was the man he had seen in McGillivray's Bar. The face had seemed familiar, and now he had his name also.

John Nicholls aka Sean Walsh aka Seamus Flynn.

Seamus Flynn. Charlie sat up, frowning. What the hell was a known IRA tearaway doing with the likes of a relatively small-time operator like Toddy Cleaver, distributing counterfeit notes?

When he left the records office James called out after him, 'Confusion to our enemies!'

I got enough of them, Charlie thought sourly.

CHAPTER 13

The physical recovery of Hannah Guderian had been remarkable. On the last occasion Eric had visited her bedside she was barely conscious; the next day he found her sitting up in bed, smiling, talking, cheerful. She recognised him immediately, which pleased him, but he had already been forewarned of the general problem.

'She's a healthy young woman and she's come through extremely well. But the mind is another thing. There's often a sort of automatic kicking-in of a memory block, when things of an unpleasant nature have occurred. It's a mental defensive mechanism, of course, and well researched. I think you will find in a day or so she will be fit to leave hospital, in a physical sense. But thereafter she'll need rest, and travelling would be unwise. I'd like to keep an eye on her for a while. Her memory of her accident may well return, but slowly.' The young doctor regarded Eric with concerned eyes. 'I understand you're her solicitor. Are you also a friend?'

'You could say that,' Eric replied guardedly.

The young doctor nodded sagely. 'I don't think the hospital environment would be the best for her, in her present condition. She's clearly not a native of this country, and I would not advise travelling any distance . . . but does she have somewhere to stay, where she could be looked after?'

'I think something could be arranged,' Eric replied.

He rang Anne at Sedleigh Hall that same morning and explained the position. She was a little guarded at first, but soon agreed to his suggestion.

Eric picked up Hannah from the hospital the next morning.

She seemed a little subdued, but otherwise in reasonable spirits, and raised no objection to the proposal he made that she stay with his ex-wife at Sedleigh Hall. As they left Newcastle and drove north she became more cheerful. It was clear she appreciated the countryside they passed through, particularly after they turned inland and began the climb into the Northumberland hills, with distant views of the sea; she observed with interest the slow-circling buzzards above them, rising on the thermals as they sought their prey on the fells below, and she exclaimed in delight as a deer with two young hinds leapt away from the lonely roadside to crash through the scattered trees that led down to a small burn. It was as though animal life had emerged to welcome her in her convalescence: they even caught sight of a red squirrel scurrying across the road in front of them. 'It's a bit like Snow White and the animals,' Eric laughed, 'but I can assure you it's not always like this. Red squirrels are rare, and I haven't seen deer on this particular stretch of road for years.'

'If I lived up here I would not wish to work in the city,' Hannah commented.

Eric hesitated. 'Well, there's a living to be earned.'

'But your wife was . . . wealthy, was she not?'

The naivete of the question gave him pause. She must have realised from his silence that she had crossed a sensitive boundary; she began to apologise but he cut her short.

'No, no, it's not necessary, Hannah. It's true that after Anne and I got married there would have been the option of my staying on the estate, busying myself with estate matters, but my interest lay in the law; I had my practice on Tyneside and while it's never been a big one, or fashionable, it's suited me.' He did not add that his attitude had caused friction over the years; Anne had never understood or accepted his need to make his own way, and she had never come to terms with the kind of business he had developed on the Quayside in Newcastle. Like his secretary, she had not approved of the nature of his client base: she was always of the view that he could have obtained a more respectable range of clients — with her assistance — in the field of corporate law. It had never appealed to him. 'I did get involved in Anne's company for a few years,' he said quietly. 'But it didn't really work out.'

And then the marriage had fallen apart. Thinking back, it was difficult now to determine just how it had gone wrong. Old tensions had faded; just who had used the wrong words in the beginning could no longer be recalled. The placid acceptance of love had slowly turned to unease, differences in viewpoint, pointless arguments, until suddenly both of them found themselves drifting in different directions.

Initially, there had been a degree of bitterness in the parting of the ways but that had been inevitable. That too had faded; their relationship now was an amicable one, based on friendship. The cicatrices of experience had become less painful, softer, fading.

'Are you sure she will welcome me?' Hannah Guderian asked uncertainly.

Eric was sure she would; at least, he *thought* he was sure. One could never tell with women.

Certainly the initial welcome was warm enough. Anne was there to meet them as they got out of the car, in front of the main entrance to Sedleigh Hall. She held Hannah by the shoulders, inspecting her face, then she laughed and gave her a warm hug. 'You didn't tell me our guest was so pretty, Eric!'

A light lunch was awaiting them; afterwards the three of them sat on the terrace overlooking the meadows and the distant Cheviots. Hannah was relaxed; she asked about the estate, commented upon the beauty of the area, but after a while it was clear she was tired so Anne suggested she might wish to rest.

After showing Hannah to her room Anne came back to the terrace where Eric still sat, sprawled in his chair. 'She seems a nice girl,' she said.

Eric glanced at her, smiling. 'I'm never quite sure what that phrase means, when one woman uses it about another.'

'She's quite beautiful.'

'She's a client,' Eric replied. 'That's all.'

Anne sat down. She was silent for a while, then she asked, 'You've not given me much detail about her. What was this accident she was involved in?'

'She was knocked down by a car. Hit and run. In Stanhope.'

'What was she doing there?'

Eric hesitated. 'It's a complicated story. I'd put her up in a hotel there.'

'Really? Why?' The puzzlement in Anne's tone was genuine, but it was underlaid by something else.

'I told you — she's just a client,' Eric insisted. 'But I felt it necessary that she should be . . . sequestered for a while. But when she came out of the hotel to make a phone call, she was knocked down.'

Anne was silent for a little while, but her eyes were fixed on him, contemplative. 'The kind of work you do, Eric, I suspect this hit and run might not have merely been an accident. In what respect are you representing her?'

He was tempted to tell her the whole story, but resisted it. He shook his head. 'Actually, I'm not really representing her. Hannah came to me for help. Then, well . . . it's rather complicated. Indeed, I'm not sure what it's all about myself.' He hesitated. 'She came north to see Dieter Barschel.'

'The man you defended?' Her eyes widened in alarm. 'The man who's been reported killed?' When Eric nodded, Anne leaned forward in her chair. 'But why did she want to see him? Is she in danger herself?'

Eric shook his head. 'Look, I don't know. I mean, she'll be safe enough here, but the police are still investigating

145

Barschel's death, and I didn't consider there would be anything gained by getting her involved. Certainly, after the accident I think in her state she's better off at Sedleigh Hall, rather than being subjected to questioning by the police. Later on, in a few days maybe, if it becomes necessary . . .'

She knew him well; she recognised there was some underlying tension in his voice. 'Are you protecting her from something, Eric?'

It was a question difficult to answer. He still could not be certain whether the running down had been an accident or something more sinister; he could not be certain that the story told to him by Jacobsen had any relevance. But she had been involved with Jacobsen; there was the matter of the missing journalist, Andrea Witt; there was the story of the Stasi death squad . . .

'Let's just say I'm taking certain precautions,' he responded.

'And this amnesia she's suffering from?' Anne pressed him.

Eric shook his head. 'It's difficult. I'll talk to her again tonight, but it seems she recalls only snatches. She recognised me when she came around; but she has no recollection of the events leading up to her accident. I've been reluctant to question her, discover exactly what she remembers, given her condition, but it's best I try soon . . .'

Hannah came down at five in the afternoon. She seemed refreshed, and Eric suggested she might enjoy a walk. He asked Anne if she would like to join them; she hesitated, but then shook her head. 'Maybe you and Hannah could use some time together, to talk.'

But she was watching Hannah carefully as they left. Eric was slightly amused at the expression on his ex-wife's face. There were not a great many years between Anne and Hannah, but Anne's concern was almost motherly.

'Anne is a very nice woman,' Hannah said soberly as they walked through the copse of trees overlooking the lake below the house. 'Some women would have been . . . concerned in such circumstances.'

'I explained you were just a client,' Eric laughed, 'if that's what you mean.'

Hannah gave him an odd look, then flushed. 'I did not mean—' As if to cover her embarrassment, she blurted out, 'It is very good of you to behave in this way, bringing me here. I recall so little of what happened. I remember going to the cottage, but then . . . I do not know. What happened?'

There was no need to burden her with all the details. They began to climb the hill towards the small meadow that lay below the crags. It had used to be a favourite walk for Eric and Anne in the old days. First there was the copse of alder and sycamore to walk through, with scattered willow and pine; then when they emerged into the meadow they would experience the rich sweet smell of the thick grass and in the distance it was possible to catch a glimpse of the sea. When the wind was in the right direction there could be the faint tang of salt in the air. 'I went down to London,' Eric admitted. 'I talked with Jacobsen.'

She stopped, turned to look at him, her eyes searching his eagerly. 'How did you know about him? I don't remember telling you—'

'I found his phone number in your apartment.' He glanced at her warily, not wishing to disturb her. 'At the cottage you'd promised to explain why you wanted to see Dieter Barschel, but after the accident you were unconscious, I needed to find out what you were involved in, so I went to see him.'

'Involved in . . .' she murmured, and then turned and began to continue the climb. 'It all seems so long ago, so vague now; he told you about my sister, Andrea?'

'He did. And he gave me the articles she wrote about the Stasi death squad.'

She nodded soberly. 'That was all it was, really. Involved . . . I loved my sister. Worshipped her, looked up to her. Andrea was so brave. So determined. She had received threats, you know, when she wrote the articles, but she went on with her research. She talked to me about what she believed, but

147

never in detail. She told me she was convinced she was on the trail of men who had done terrible things years ago. Men who were now cloaked in respectability, but who were still doing evil things. And then, one night, she merely disappeared.' Her head was down, a deep frown on her forehead. 'I looked for her. I went to the police. But though they helped initially, soon they just shook their heads, closed the files, walked away from the whole thing. In Germany, there are people still who wish to forget what happened in East Germany those years ago. They want it erased. They don't want to accept what my sister had once written: *these people were trained to make murders look like accidents or suicides, even ordinary crimes such as robberies.* So a man hanging himself in prison, another suffocated in a cell, someone drowning in a car in a canal, seemingly drunk; an unexplained disappearance here, an overdose of barbiturates there . . . The police investigate, shrug their shoulders, turn their backs . . . but I could not do that.'

She turned her head to look at Eric. 'I *needed* to find out what had happened to Andrea.'

'You got hold of her files,' Eric said.

Hannah nodded. They had reached the top of the hill; the sunlight lay warm on the lush grass of the meadow. On the heather-strewn hill sloping above them, up to the crag, they heard the rattling, whirring sound of a cock pheasant. Eric gestured towards a stone seat that he and Anne had caused to be placed at the foot of the slope, years ago. From there they could enjoy the sun on their faces, and the distant blue line of the sea.

Hannah sat down, put her head back, half-closed her eyes against the sun.

'I talked to many people in Germany, including the editors who had published Andrea's work. It was strange. They were sympathetic, helpful up to a point. But underlying their words I detected a reluctance. They wanted to . . . how do you say? Let sleeping dogs lie. I got the impression they felt it was unwise to expose such things, turn over too many stones . . . Finally, I came to England. I had been given Mr Jacobsen's name: he had corresponded with Andrea when she was writing for *Bild*. I had come to a dead end. I wanted to find out if he could give me anything more. It was he who mentioned Dieter Barschel.'

'In what context?' Eric asked.

'The Stasi. In his view, as a young, impressionable man, Barschel had been recruited as a Stasi informant. He was recruited when he was in the junior football squad of Dynamo Berlin. Later, he was encouraged to move to Italy, and elsewhere: during these changes, he continued to work for the Stasi secret police. It was all in the past, of course. But Mr Jacobsen had followed his career in England. He suggested that maybe Barschel would be worth talking to. It was vague, uncertain, I was not sure how Barschel could help me . . . but I was at the end of my road. There were no more turnings. So many dead ends. I was getting nowhere. So I came north. And now . . . it is finished. I have no other place to go: no avenues to explore. Andrea had disappeared. So I tried to meet Dieter Barschel. And now he too is dead.'

She glanced at Eric; her eyes were troubled. 'I was confused. I didn't want to be involved. Was I wrong to ask you to take me away?'

Eric hesitated. 'I don't know. I don't see it makes any difference, really. There's no information you could have given the police that they now don't have. Apart, maybe, from Barschel's previous links with the Stasi — but that was a long time ago. I think it best to stay out of it, at least for the time being. Later perhaps, I'll talk to them . . . Don't worry. If you do talk to them eventually, I'll explain the delay was the result of my advice, as your lawyer. After seeing Jacobsen . . . well, in any case there is a policeman who has the information. He was with me in London.'

She hardly seemed to be listening. Her gaze was vacant as she stared out across the meadow. 'I know now I will never find out what happened to her. My dear sister is dead, I am certain. And I will never know how; or be able to bury her.'

A single tear trickled down her cheek. Eric took her hand. They sat there side by side in the sunlight, each busy with their individual thoughts. For Hannah Guderian it was sadness at the memory of the half-sister she had lost. For Eric, it was the uneasy thought that Charlie Spate might have the information about the Stasi death squad, but in his present state of mind there was the likelihood that he was not handing it over to his colleagues, for reasons of his own.

* * *

Charlie Spate had thought about it for a long time. He was aware he was treading on thin ice. He was unable to determine how important Jacobsen's information actually was since it contained few hard facts — mainly suppositions. The writings of a journalist who had disappeared; the hunt by Hannah Guderian for information that might lead to an answer to her questions. And Dieter Barschel had had his head blown off.

The Barschel case was in the hands of Inspector Joe Martin: he had not spoken to Charlie about it and in his present situation Charlie was disinclined to approach him. He had been formally told to stay away, under suspension, so he had that excuse to avoid Martin. At the same time he could not remain passively accepting of his suspension — he needed to do something to weaken Charteris's case against him.

And now he had a key to his problem. He could use Elaine Start's investigation to get back into business. He had already surprised her with the revelation that he knew about Toddy Cleaver. But that wasn't enough: she had still warned him off, if only for his own sake. But now, maybe he had something else — another piece to fit into a confusing jigsaw.

Elaine had recently acquired a small semi-detached house in Westerhope, not far from the airport at Ponteland. She lived alone. Charlie took the Metro out of the city. There was the chance, after he'd talked to her, she'd give him a lift home. You never knew your luck.

It was only a short walk from the Metro station to the small estate on which she lived. He had already checked to determine whether she was off duty. He found the house easily enough, located in a quiet cul-de-sac, and rang the bell. There was a short delay; he looked about him. The sky was clear, stars sharp in the evening sky. The door opened. She stood there looking at him expressionlessly. She wore a shapeless jogging suit, with baggy, faded pants, unlaced trainers on her feet.

'Been running?' he asked cheerfully.

'Watching television. In comfortable clothes.' She cocked a suspicious eyebrow. 'What do you want, DCI Spate?'

'Off duty it's Charlie, Elaine.'

'Not until I know what you're here for,' she said coolly.

'I've got another name to give you,' Charlie replied. 'And I bet you're enjoying a drink, while you're watching television.' She stood there staring at him for several moments, clearly uncertain what to do. Then she shook her head wearily, clucked her tongue. 'I've seen the damn film anyway. You better come in.'

He followed her, closing the door behind him. The sitting room was comfortably furnished, illuminated by a single standard lamp. The film she had been watching was a Western of some vintage. At least fifty years old, he guessed. He remembered now, she was a bit of a film buff. 'Good film?'

Winchester '73. About a dogged character who just won't let go. In his case, he wanted to get back a rifle. What's it in your case, Charlie? You know you shouldn't be here. You know you should be staying away from any case currently under investigation. So why won't you let go?'

'Maybe because I'm public-spirited. I want to help.'

She hesitated, then walked over to the settee, picked up the control box and clicked off the television. 'I'm drinking gin and tonic,' she muttered.

'A woman's drink. But I'll settle for the same, unless you've got whisky.' Without invitation, he headed for the settee, slumped down, spread his arms wide along the back. At the sideboard Elaine Start poured him a glass of Famous

Grouse. She came back to the settee, handed him the glass, shook her head at the ease in which he had established himself on the settee, and then pointedly sat in the easy chair at least five feet distant, facing him. 'So,' she said, 'you were saying you have another name for me.'

'This investigation into the counterfeiting,' he asked, admiring the depth of colour in the whisky he held in his left hand, 'does it have any political connections?'

'How do you mean?'

'Well, from what you told me earlier, the Garda have identified these Flaherty lads in Dublin as a criminal organisation, linking up with people in Middlesbrough, and now Newcastle — through Toddy Cleaver — to distribute the notes here on the mainland.'

'That's right,' Elaine agreed carefully.

'And the Garda haven't suggested there's any other involvement of a *political* nature?'

'Get on with it, Charlie.'

'They haven't suggested any IRA involvement?'

She heaved a sigh. 'Get real, Charlie. There are villains in Ireland who don't necessarily have the backing of the IRA. OK, the politicians have been having a field day over the involvement of IRA gangs in bank robberies, and the peace agreement has foundered, with Sinn Fein screaming it's all nothing to do with them, but there's no evidence that this little scam has any connection at all with the nationalists. It's just a simple, effective money-making operation.'

'Yet I've got another name to give you.'

She sipped her gin and tonic, eyeing him carefully. 'So, give it to me. Let me see if it rings a bell.'

'Seamus Flynn.'

There was a long silence. Elaine Start shook her head. 'Not a clang.'

'You don't even know who he is? Well, I do. I've looked him up. You'll probably know something about the Derry riots in 1972 and the Bloody Sunday killings, even if they were before your time. You should do because it's stayed in the news ever since. Over the years all forces have been getting updates and review information from the Home Office as more news gets churned out by the media and the Intelligence people pick up more that they can divulge without jeopardising their activities. The latest is the search for the weapons actually used by the paratroopers on the day in question. The investigators have been chasing them all over the world, without much success after the Ministry of Defence decommissioned them and sold them on to Lebanon's paramilitary Internal Security Force, and to West Africa, to bandits like the bloody drug-addled West Side Boys. Anything for money, it seems.'

'I'm still not getting your point.'

'I've ploughed through some of the Home Office circulars. They were largely based on Europol information. Some of them relate to a problem the investigators were hitting. They were trying to track down twenty-nine SLRs — self-loading rifles used by the troops that day. But they faced considerable delays — and they got bogged down by legal issues raised by a group of lawyers in Ireland, who were being particularly obstructive. The Home Office believed they too were after these weapons, for the propaganda effect they would have if they announced their discovery.'

'What does this have to do with—'

'Patience, DS Start, patience,' Charlie pleaded, holding up a hand. 'It then became apparent that the group also had very close contacts with some of the more militant offshoots of the IRA, and that three of them in particular could be tied in to a bank raid across the border which resulted in the death of a bank clerk. One of the men concerned was Seamus Flynn.'

Elaine grimaced, sipped at her gin and tonic and crossed one leg over the other. Charlie wished she had been wearing a skirt. 'You can identify this man?' she asked.

'I've seen his mug shot in the Europol files at the station. More important, I've seen him here on Tyneside.' Her eyes widened. 'Even so, to link him with—'

'My informant—' Charlie had a brief memory of Calico Jim with his battered dungaree cap and bleary eyes, '—he tells me that Seamus Flynn has some kind of deal going with Toddy Cleaver. If that's the case, maybe you should be looking to request the Garda to reopen their terrorist file. It may be this isn't a straightforward counterfeiting scam.'

'Or maybe your Seamus Flynn has discarded his old political coat, and is now just about making a dollar or two on his own account. Anyway . . .' She hesitated, clearly undecided whether she should confide in him. 'It looks as though we'll find out pretty soon.'

'How do you mean?'

She smiled, almost catlike as she slipped off her trainers and curled herself up in her chair. 'It's all going to happen tomorrow night. There's a shipment of notes coming in along the river. We'll be there to meet it.'

'If Flynn's involved he could slip the net, you wouldn't recognise him,' Charlie Spate urged. 'Let me come along—'

Elaine clearly thought that it was a bad idea. 'DCI Spate, if Charteris found out . . .'

'I'm certainly not going to tell him!'

She hesitated, mulled the thought over a little longer. 'On the other hand, I suppose if you stay out of the limelight, do an imitation of a back-up from the shadows . . .'

'Tell me when and where,' he urged, 'and I'll be there.'

She was hesitant still, but he knew she was going to agree. She glanced at her watch, thought for a little while.

'Charlie, it's getting late. Are you hoping for a lift home tonight?' she asked.

He grinned. 'I was thinking along those lines.'

'Forget it,' she said.

CHAPTER 14

Charlie had thought he was on to a good thing. He'd thought he'd finally cracked the nut: he'd be staying the night.

But that wasn't the way it turned out. Elaine Start had known for a long time that Charlie had lusted after her. He guessed there were times when she had seriously thought about acknowledging his desires by doing something about them — like capitulation. And for a while, last night, it had looked that way. As she had walked past him to replenish her glass he had grabbed her hand and done his forceful masculine thing, pulling her down onto the settee beside him, fastening his mouth on hers, and clamping one hand on one of the breasts he had admired so much, pinning one of her thighs with his. She had clearly discarded her bra for comfort before he arrived, so in a moment he was able to give her the full treatment.

And there had been signs that the attack was working. He had recognised definite intimations of stimulation and there had been a considerable response to his kiss. But when he came up for breath, she had pulled back her head and looked him straight in the eye.

'DCI Spate, do you want to tell me now what you got up to with that tart Romy Arendt?'

The unexpected question had pricked the bubble of his ego and lustful thoughts had fled. And, it turned out, when she had earlier told him to forget about her giving him a lift the comment was designed to tell him he'd have to call a cab. It had never been an invitation to stay the night.

Nevertheless, after she had rearranged herself back in the easy chair, with a fresh drink, it gave them the opportunity to be frank with each other.

He'd given her the full details about the way he'd been conned by the Arendt woman, though he'd left out most of the lascivious bits, and when he explained that the liaison had largely been due to his secret thoughts about Elaine Start herself, and his lack of success in obtaining any favourable response, she had looked startled at first, but then seemed to have accepted it as a reasonable statement of some veracity.

'Knowing the way your mind works,' she had conceded.

It meant also that he could stay there a bit longer — though with fading hopes of success — while they talked about the set-up, the arrest, and the mystery of why Dieter Barschel had to die.

'I can't really see the connection,' Elaine had admitted. 'Cleaver employs Barschel as a runner, working with the bookies at the track. *Someone* sets Barschel up, using your . . . connection with Romy Arendt, and plants drugs on him. So is this just to get him out of the way for a while? It would hardly be Cleaver who set him up — the guy's working for him, after all. Then you get screwed in court, Barschel walks out on bail and soon after must have wished he'd stayed nice and safe in the lock-up.'

'Does Inspector Martin have any leads?'

Elaine grimaced. 'He's not saying much, but I think that's because he hasn't got a lot. I handed the files over to him and we've had a chat, he's rounding up the usual suspects as they say, but so far he's getting nowhere.'

'Did you give him Toddy Cleaver's name?'

She was silent for a little while, gnawing at her lower lip in discomfort. 'I couldn't do that.'

'Not even after I told you Barschel was a runner for him?' Elaine detected the sneer in Charlie's tone and reacted angrily. 'I didn't want to talk to him about Cleaver until we'd done the deal on the counterfeit ring! If I'd given Inspector Martin the link he'd have pulled Cleaver in, and that could have blown the operation we're running with Cleveland and the Garda! Our business could be winding up tomorrow night, and I can give Joe Martin Cleaver's name then. But at the moment . . .'

'Withholding evidence from your own colleagues,' Charlie mocked.

'Not as bad as sleeping with a whore who then turns you over,' she retaliated.

Charlie held up a hand. 'All right, all right, an armistice, right? But anyway, it looks as though Cleaver and Seamus Flynn are involved in this counterfeiting business — my guess would be it was Flynn who made the link for Cleaver with the Flaherty gang. As for Dieter Barschel . . .'

Charlie hesitated. He had just mocked Elaine Start for failing to give Inspector Martin useful information in his investigation into the murder of Dieter Barschel, but Charlie was guilty of the same thing. He had not told Elaine about Hannah Guderian and her search for the truth of her half-sister's disappearance. It was true he'd given his word to Eric Ward, who himself had been guilty of holding back evidence when he had failed to disclose the fact that the Guderian woman had been with him when he discovered the body at the cottage, but he wasn't above breaking that promise. On the other hand, he had the feeling it was something he should hold back, a card unseen in his hand, a bargaining counter later when he had to face the enquiry that Charteris was keen on setting up. He couldn't tell right now how it might help, but he was working on instinct, a gut feeling. Besides, it didn't seem to fit in anywhere, this story of a missing journalist, her half-sister's quest, and German newspaper hysteria about a Stasi death squad that had existed twenty years ago.

Now, a day later, as he lay on the grassy bank high above the deserted quayside, Charlie thrust aside all the thoughts crowding into his head, about the peremptory way in which Elaine had thrown him out without even a goodnight kiss after calling a cab, about the mystery of Dieter Barschel's death, the running down of Hannah Guderian, and the stories of an East German secret police force that might or might not have re-emerged. He had to concentrate on what was happening below. He glanced at his watch. Elaine Start's timetable had suggested her task force would be in place at midnight, to await the arrival of the motor launch from Middlesbrough, expected in the early hours.

The trouble was the boat was already docked at the quayside.

The building of the Millennium Bridge, the refurbishment of the old warehouse to create the arts complex at the Baltic Centre, and the erection of the reflective-roofed Sage music centre had transformed the Gateshead bank, fighting to challenge its Newcastle rival for glitter, excitement and leisure pursuits. It was resulting in other developments, the creation of new apartment blocks, the regeneration of the banks fronting the river, hotels, clubs — more amenities for the residents, and in due course no doubt, Charlie thought sourly, more problems for the police.

The immediate consequence of all the activity was that swathes of the riverbank had been changed, houses demolished, factories pulled down, warehouses gutted for redevelopment.

It had been necessary to clear areas fronting on the river in accordance with some grand master plan in the local authority office; tenders had been made, plans approved, and work had commenced. But the result for some areas was that while dockyard facilities remained there was no shipping activity there, now that the factories had gone. Fenced off with high wire and padlocked gates, there were some stretches of quayside which were derelict, awaiting redevelopment. One such was the short stretch of quay area that Charlie was observing: Morden Landing.

There had been some degree of vandalism, almost inevitably. Although the factory had been demolished, with just a few walls and heaps of rubble now to be seen, young tearaways learning their trade had broken the locks on the gates, pulled down some of the fencing, ranged around the premises finding nothing of value and consequently undertaking further wrecking operations. The area was like a war zone, but was now deserted, left to its own devices, and Charlie had watched from the bank as the motor launch had slipped in at Morden Landing, smooth, sleek, powerful engines purring. At least three hours early.

When Elaine had grudgingly allowed that Charlie could come out provided he remained on the fringe of the action it gave him licence to do his own thing. In his experience operations like this often failed to go to order; Elaine's planning had been tight, dependent as it was upon the information coming in from the liaison officer in Cleveland. They were to inform her when the suspect vessel was to set out for the Tyne; only then would the Tyneside task force take up positions to await the arrival of the vessel. But clearly, something had gone wrong. The motor launch had already arrived.

Elaine had explained the plan to him, as they sat with their drinks at her house. 'From the information we've had, the launch will be loaded at Middlesbrough and then track up to the Tyne. There's to be a lorry waiting to unload the notes, coming in from the north to Morden Landing. We'll be setting up a road block to intercept the lorry before the contact can be made. We don't want some crazy chase through the Northumberland countryside. So, first, we pick up the lorry. Then, almost immediately, we'll move in on the boat. If we time it right there won't be opportunity for them to cast off and head out to sea, where they could dump the cargo and claim they were clean. The timing is all important, of course. If we hit them quickly enough, there shouldn't be too much trouble.'

But somehow, the intelligence had gone wrong. The boat was already in, and Charlie was aware of movement in the area.

From his vantage point, and with a pair of night sight binoculars, Charlie watched with interest.

First, some twenty minutes after the boat had docked the car had come over the hill, its headlights dipped, then switched off entirely as it coasted down to a position some two hundred yards from Morden Landing. It remained there, dark in colour, barely visible, silent. After a short delay Charlie became aware of movement on the boat itself. Three men came out on deck; they remained there for a short while, and then stepped down from the boat, casually, strolling along towards the damaged gates of the factory landing. There was some laughter, one pushed another in retaliation for some kind of joke, and then the three men strolled onwards towards town. It was not a long walk, and they were in no great hurry. One stopped, lit a cigarette and then re-joined his companions. Charlie guessed they were crewmen. Their job done, maybe paid off, they were headed for town, maybe a late drink in a nightclub. The sound of their voices came to him; he could not make out the words, but the sounds soon faded to a murmur, and then he could hear nothing as the crewmen disappeared from sight.

He switched the binoculars back to the car. He could see no one inside; the car windows seemed dark, opaque. Then, after a few minutes, the car doors opened, there was a brief flash of light. Two men emerged: at this distance Charlie could not make out their faces but one was considerably taller than the other, broad-shouldered, deliberate in his movements. The smaller man moved in quick, excited, jerky steps. He led the way towards the ruined gates, and Morden Landing.

Charlie watched as they climbed aboard. He checked his watch. There was still no sign of Elaine's task force. Charlie waited, continued to watch the boat. The night air was cool on his skin; he was sweating, nervous. Something had gone wrong, he was certain of it. Elaine should be here by now. The wind rose suddenly, a gusting breeze coming in from the sea. The river's gurgle reached him on the breeze, a plopping sound carried on the night air.

In a little while there was further movement on the boat. One man came out on the deck; it was the big, broad-shouldered man. He raised his head, as though sniffing the air. He stepped down from the deck awkwardly, burdened by what he carried. It was long, and as far as Charlie could make out with the night light, swathed in a shiny material, like oiled canvas. The big man moved purposefully towards the car in the shadows. He opened the door, got into the driving seat, but again the brief flash of the car's interior light enabled Charlie to make out little. The car's engine rumbled into life. The driver made a slow careful turn and headed back up the hill. In moments it was gone; there was a brief flash of headlights, and then the darkness flooded back in once more.

Charlie concentrated on the boat, grimacing his uncertainty. Where the hell was Elaine and her troops?

Slowly he rose to his feet, his dark clothes blending against the hillside. There was no movement from the boat. He was troubled; things had not gone to plan. He hesitated, and finally took out his mobile phone.

Elaine Start answered after a short delay. 'Where the hell are you?' Charlie demanded.

Her tone sounded weary. 'I ought to be in bed, instead of writing out a bloody report. Where are you?'

'At Morden Landing for God's sake. Like we planned!'

She gave a sigh. 'I'm sorry, Charlie, I should have contacted you, but I was so angry, and I had to stand down everyone, and there's all hell on here with arguments about the waste of time—'

'What the hell are you talking about?' he snarled in fury.

'All right, all right, Charlie calm down,' she snapped. 'So you've had a cold wait on the hill and I'm bloody furious but so what? We've both been buggered about.'

'Gimme the story,' Charlie demanded.

He heard her sigh. 'You know we've been liaising with Cleveland. Most of our intelligence has come from them, and the Garda in Dublin. You know what was due to happen — I told you about it, the lorry, the task force, the raid on the boat once it arrived at Morden Landing. Cleveland's main source has been a customs officer who they had over a barrel for corruption — cigarette and booze smuggling, if you can believe it.' She sighed again, wearily. 'Anyway, this evening the message came through. There'd be no run of the counterfeit notes to Tyneside: Cleveland had said they'd had an anonymous tip-off, decided to go with it, believing it wasn't worth the risk to delay, they say. Me, I suspect it was all a matter of pride. They wanted to make the collar themselves. So much for bloody liaison. They raided the warehouse at Monkwearmouth where the stuff was being held. They've pulled in the whole group. End of story. Except that we're left dangling at our end. We'll get a load of thanks for our cooperation, of course, but when I put in my report to Charteris I somehow get the feeling it will all end up on my plate. The blame, I mean.'

Charlie felt cold. He turned, stared at the silent boat moored at Morden Landing. 'Never mind the blame,' he said. 'Something's gone wrong.'

'I know,' she replied, irritably, 'I was just telling you, those bloody people in Cleveland—'

'No, listen to me,' Charlie insisted. 'Whatever's gone wrong in Cleveland, I wouldn't know about. But the boat's here!'

There was a short silence. 'What the hell are you talking about, DCI Spate?'

'You told me you were expecting a boat in here tonight. Well, whatever's gone down in Monkwearmouth, I'm telling you the boat is here, DS Start. I'm still on suspension and I'd better keep out of this so you'd better get down here as quick as the proverbial bat out of hell!'

Elaine Start's car came over the hill just twenty minutes later. Still at his vantage point, watching the boat, Charlie scrambled down over the tussocks of grass and rocky scree that littered the slope and was waiting at the foot of the hill outside the wrecked gates when she pulled up in front of him. When she got out he remarked, 'So you didn't bring the cavalry, then.'

She was not amused. 'After standing them down? All those macho guys with their body armour, face helmets, riot sticks and the odd weapon or two? They went away talking blue murder about women police officers, started checking in their weapons, grumbling all the way about organising piss-ups in breweries and I had to take it all! No, not a chance of calling them out again. Besides . . .' She looked past him to the dark, sleek boat lying quietly at Morden Landing. 'I couldn't be certain you knew what you were talking about.'

'Seeing is believing, DS Start,' Charlie muttered caustically.

'Everything's quiet.'

'As the grave. I saw the crew leave. Two guys then went on board. One of them left. That's when I called you, because there was no sign of the task force and I had no idea what the hell was going on.'

'Not a lot, it seems,' she murmured. 'I don't see how I can call for back-up . . .'

Charlie shrugged. 'We just do our duty as conscientious, committed police officers,' he said drily. 'You say there's been no counterfeit notes run, so we're just looking over a boat that seems to be minding its own business, but in an out-of-the-way place. Nothing wrong with that.'

'Charlie—'

'With what's been going on, there'll just be the one man on board. Maybe got his head down by now; sleeping the sleep of the honest citizen. So, let's take a look.'

She hesitated, then nodded. Charlie led the way. They walked through the gates, crossed the littered dock. Charlie climbed up onto the deck, gave Elaine a hand, hauling her aboard. Silence greeted them. Charlie walked forward, opened the door to the hatchway. The boat rocked quietly as ripples came in from the far bank; in the distance Charlie heard the mournful sound of a siren. Elaine was close behind him as he moved forward; the deck was dark, and he moved carefully down the companionway. He heard Elaine fumbling behind him, and she brought out her flashlight.

The beam cut across the cabin area in front of them. It gleamed on the windows, reflecting back at them; it picked out the plush seating that ran along either side. It wavered, then stopped, focusing on the blood that was staining the seat, and the hand that still seemed to be clinging limply to the bulwark for support. Charlie took the flashlight from his companion and stepped forward. The bullet had entered the man's forehead, a neat hole. It would be a different matter at the back of the head: the exit wound would be horrific. Behind him, Elaine was breathing hard as he played the flashlight over the man's sandy hair. 'Do you know him?' Charlie asked.

'It's Toddy Cleaver,' she replied, in a shaky voice. 'But Charlie, I think there's another one . . .'

Charlie flashed the beam around the cabin. She was right. But this one had taken the bullet in the throat. He had died messily, and slowly. The life had gradually pumped out of him, as he choked from the suffusion of blood that had flooded over his shoulders and chest. The dark stains seemed to have spread everywhere. 'You identified Cleaver,' Charlie said. 'This one is someone I recognise. Cleaver's partner in crime.'

'Who—'

'Our Irish friend,' Charlie interrupted brusquely. 'Seamus Flynn.' Suddenly, he was in charge again, confident. 'DS Start, you'd better get on your phone. Now; we need back-up. Meanwhile, you know the score. We need the forensic team out here before we touch anything.'

She stepped back towards the companionway, climbed up onto the deck and he heard her radio in. Charlie stood where he was, staring at the distorted features of Seamus Flynn. There had been a neatness in the way that Toddy Cleaver had died: a single shot to the centre of the forehead. Precise. But Flynn had died more slowly. The throat wound would have kept him quiet, apart from the gurgling. A slower death. Malice.

Elaine stood at the top of the companionway. 'They're on their way,' she said woodenly.

Charlie nodded. He was curious. None of this made sense to him. Then he thought back to the man he had seen arrive, and then leave. He'd been carrying something. Charlie hesitated, then moved forward along the cabin to the door at the far end. It led to the berths. He opened the door. Shone the flashlight inside. There were two packing cases on the deck floor. One of them had been opened, its lid thrust to one side. He caught a glimpse, a dull metallic gleam.

'DS Start, you'd better come see this.'

She clattered down the companionway. She saw him standing in the doorway and moved to join him. 'You found the money? The counterfeit notes?'

He glanced back at her, then stood aside so she could see. 'No. Not money.' He fixed the beam on the contents of the packing case. 'Not counterfeit money. Guns.'

CHAPTER 15

To say that ACC Charteris was displeased was putting it mildly. Enraged, Charlie thought, was a better word.

Elaine had been the first to face the ACC's fury; Charlie was the second to be marched in. 'You were *suspended*, Spate,' Charteris bellowed. 'You deliberately disobeyed my orders. You've been interfering with current investigations, putting them at risk—'

'I don't see it that way, sir,' Charlie had defended himself. 'If I hadn't been on surveillance—'

'Which you *shouldn't* have been,' Charteris snarled unpleasantly.

'—who knows how long that boat could have been moored at Morden Landing before someone climbed aboard, kids maybe, who would've trampled all over the place, fouled up the forensics. How long till we found those bodies? How long—'

'How long before I get through your thick skull that this is a police force not a private detective agency where people can run around doing just as they please! All right, I concede if you hadn't been there it would have been some time before we would have been able to get the forensic team in there; days during which evidence could have been lost, defiled,

166

the hell knows what! But that doesn't negate the point I'm making! You were on bloody *suspension*!' Charteris stopped, his handsome features distorted with anger and injured pride. He made a deliberate effort to calm down, regain control. 'In the meantime, I've got to decide what to do. This is developing into something akin to a charnel house! I've got one investigation running on the murder of this Barschel character, and Inspector Martin seems to be getting nowhere bloody fast. The counterfeiting operation has blown up in our faces: the Cleveland people will take all the credit. And now we've got two more corpses to account for. I want to know what the hell is going on!'

'Don't forget the guns, sir,' Charlie reminded him, with a hint of malice.

Charteris didn't appreciate the reminder. He glowered at Charlie. 'Well that's one thing at least we can hand over to someone else. I'll be calling in some Home Office experts to handle that.'

Charlie was puzzled. 'Why do that, sir?'

Charteris grimaced. 'From what I now hear you've been buggering around on your own account, poking your suspended nose in here and there, including rummaging through Home Office files we keep on record. Well, one thing's for sure — you didn't read up all you could have done. There's a recent confidential circular you'll have missed.'

'And what might that be, sir?'

Charteris didn't like Charlie's tone, and he scowled, close to losing his temper again. 'There's a directive concerning an Intelligence report about the recent agreement between various parties on decommissioning.'

Charlie's eyes widened. 'The peace agreement?'

'If you can call it that,' Charteris replied sourly. 'The directive warns that particular attention should be paid to the recovery of identifiable arms that should be handed over, or destroyed under the peace agreement, but which might not be accounted for.'

Charlie frowned. 'I'm not certain what—'

'Army Intelligence suggests that following on the peace agreement, when decommissioning finally goes through, and the IRA openly destroy their arms — and get the events verified — it's highly likely that certain maverick elements within the organisation will seek to turn the events into private profits. Who the hell knows just how many arms are held by the IRA? They've been buying stuff in for years, stockpiling it in various hideaways south of the border for decades. No doubt in due course they'll make a show of it, destroying arms left right and centre in the presence of a designated inspector — but will they show everything? I doubt it, and the Intelligence services are certain about it. Since we don't know how many caches they've really got, some of the stockpile will go missing. So the discovery of these arms on that bloody boat means I'm calling in the experts. They'll be able to tell what the provenance of these guns are.'

He hesitated, his face twisting with displeasure. He didn't like saying what he was about to say. 'And of course, your identification of that bastard Seamus Flynn helps. He was well known to have IRA connections.'

Charlie raised his chin defiantly. 'What I don't quite understand, sir, is that Flynn was identified in the Home Office circular some time ago. All forces were told to keep an eye open for him. But when I saw him, large as life in McGillivray's Bar, he was enjoying himself quite openly among a group of Irish friends. I haven't been around here long enough to know but why wasn't he picked up before now?'

Charteris bristled. 'Policy, Spate, policy. You've seen what's been happening since the Good Friday Agreement. The government's been soft-pedalling. The pressure's been off Sinn Fein, men have been released from prison, all in the name of establishing a proper democratic future for the whole of Ireland. In other words, we were told the heat was off. Men like Flynn weren't to be harassed. Clearly, for him, it simply meant he could wander around openly while he was still making use of the contacts he'd made on Tyneside to go into business for himself. Selling guns that should have been decommissioned. But all that's beside the point. The arms will be handed over to Home Office investigators. The question we have to answer now is: who ended the careers of Flynn and Toddy Cleaver?'

'I could suggest an answer, sir.'

ACC Charteris peered at Charlie suspiciously. 'No doubt you've been thinking hard about this ever since you found the bodies,' he sneered.

Charlie ignored the jibe. 'Going back to the counterfeiting ring, and the liaison with Cleveland and Dublin, I understand you've also been receiving assistance of late from a prominent . . . *businessman*, you call him?'

ACC Charteris stiffened, and glared at Charlie. 'What's that supposed to mean?'

'I'm talking about Mark Vasagar. It's common knowledge he's taken over much of the organised crime along the river, after striking a deal with his predecessor Mad Jack Tenby.'

Charteris sniffed contemptuously. 'It's *your* theory, at least, and one we've heard more than a little of this last two years.'

'But while Vasagar is pretty much in control, he's still relatively new to the business here. There'll be a lot of people who'll be nibbling away at the edges, testing the strength of Vasagar's commitment, wanting to get a slice of the action without paying their dues to the club, so to speak.'

'And you think—'

'It's worth putting money on, sir,' Charlie insisted. 'I've been told that in the course of the joint investigation between ourselves, Cleveland and Dublin, into the distribution of counterfeit notes throughout the north-east, Mark Vasagar has been helpful, providing us with useful information. A villain like Vasagar does nothing for reasons of public service, you and I know that. So what does he get out of it?' Charlie hesitated. 'I gather the striking of a deal of some kind with Vasagar was approved at a high level. *Sir.*'

For a moment Charlie thought he had gone too far. ACC Charteris paled; there was an angry line to his mouth and his eyes were stained with venom. 'There's been no deal with Vasagar, DCI Spate,' he insisted in a cold voice.

None that could be openly acknowledged, Charlie thought. Doggedly, he went on, 'Deal or no deal, it stands to reason that Vasagar isn't going to help us on breaking a counterfeit ring unless there's something in it for him. That can mean, in my book, just one thing.'

'And what may that be?' Charteris sneered.

'Consolidation. Tightening his grip on the river rats. Making sure no operations of any size come in without his sanction.'

'You've got no proof—'

'But it stands to reason. Mark Vasagar gets wind of the fact that there's a ring operating on his patch. He's got no slice of the action; he doesn't like that. He's got choices: do nothing — which is a non-starter — sort the matter out himself, or when he hears there's a police operation out to catch the villains, cooperate with us.'

There was a short silence. ACC Charteris was staring at Charlie contemplatively. He was lost in thought for a little while. Then he nodded, 'All right. Conceding that your theory makes sense . . .' Abruptly, he turned to his desk, picked up the phone. 'I want DS Start back in here. Now.'

The two men waited in the ensuing silence. Charlie remained standing, the palms of his hands sweating. Charteris behaved as though he was not there. Seated behind his desk he began to read a report, though Charlie suspected his mind was still clicking on with what had been said. He had no doubt, personally, that Charteris had been involved in sanctioning an arrangement with Vasagar, though he guessed he would never get to know the nature of the deal. Also, now that Charlie had planted seeds of doubt in his mind about the nature of the agreement, and the motivation behind it as far as Vasagar was concerned, Charteris had to do something to check. He could not afford to be exposed in this way, not with the glittering career he had mapped out for himself placed at risk. If Charteris were to be shown to have been fooled in his dealings by a smooth-faced villain, his reputation would be shredded. He was not about to let that happen.

There was a tap on the door, Charteris called out, and DS Elaine Start came into the room. She walked forward to stand beside Charlie, shoulder to shoulder. He liked that. It displayed a sort of loyalty. Charteris looked up, observed them sourly. 'DCI Spate here, on suspension, was allowed to get involved with an investigation under your control, DS Start. That was in clear breach of my orders, and a matter of disciplinary action. As I informed you a little while ago, I'll be considering what to do about that in due course, but meanwhile DCI Spate has drawn my attention to the source of some of the information you've been receiving.'

'Sir?' Elaine Start tensed, uncertain.

'From Mark Vasagar.'

Elaine Start stiffened, shot a quick, resentful glance at Charlie. 'There have been two meetings with Mr Vasagar,' she admitted. 'The information he gave us was very useful. It was he who gave us the name of Toddy Cleaver—'

'Who has since passed away, not quite peacefully, on the boat,' Charlie intervened.

Elaine Start swallowed. Her tone was muffled with anger. 'He also confirmed that Cleaver was working the racecourse. He gave us the link over the counterfeiting distribution. So, when we'd conferred with Cleveland, as you'd requested, sir, and the intelligence came in from Dublin, it was clear he was giving us sound information.'

'Was it Vasagar,' Charlie interrupted, 'who gave you the information about time and place of the delivery at Morden Landing?'

Elaine Start took a deep breath. 'We were told by Cleveland liaison that the shipment of notes had arrived and were to be held in Monkwearmouth until a consignment was delivered to the Tyne. I . . . I caused a check to be made with Mr Vasagar, and was informed that his sources confirmed that the delivery was to be made. He did not specify the time—'

'What about the place?' Charlie asked.

She nodded. 'He told us it would be Morden Landing. I got in touch with Cleveland; they agreed to check their contacts, and then later said it looked as though the shipment would be leaving Monkwearmouth last night. So I made the necessary arrangements. You'll recall sir that it was you who backed the involvement of the task force, the issue of arms—'

'Which later had to be rescinded when we were told Cleveland had received a tip-off that plans were changed.'

'Vasagar again?' Charlie sneered.

'They felt they could wait no longer, and moved in to arrest the gang,' Charteris muttered, sending Charlie a murderous look. 'All right . . .' His reptilian glance moved to Charlie. 'Things have gone haywire around here. And I'm short, as always, of qualified manpower. We're getting nowhere with the killing of Dieter Barschel. It may be the counterfeit ring has been sorted but in its place we've got another two corpses on our hands. And two packing cases full of SA80 standard army infantry rifles. God knows where they came from. The Home Office experts will tell us, eventually. But when you were expecting dud notes on that boat, you got rifles and how the hell do you explain that?'

'If you want my opinion, sir, Seamus Flynn is the key,' Charlie announced. 'The whisper was that Cleaver and Flynn were involved in the distribution of the notes, fine; but I think some of the information that came in was flawed. It may be Flynn was involved in the counterfeit operation but we have to remember Flynn would have had other opportunities from his old contacts in Ireland. Maybe he was just tapping into a system already set up to bring in the dud notes, but was really more interested in using the same system to bring in the guns. I don't know whether Vasagar knew about it: maybe he did but kept quiet about it. Maybe he was intending taking the guns from Flynn, or had even struck a deal with him.' Charlie flashed a quick glance at Elaine. 'He never gave us a time for the pick-up, did he? Just the place. Maybe Vasagar's idea was to get the guns away before your task force arrived.'

Elaine Start faced him. 'The timing would have been too tight, surely.'

'Why?' Charlie asked, glaring at her, exuding confidence now. 'If he was working with you, feeding you information, why couldn't he have a contact in Cleveland? My guess is, sir,' he insisted, turning back to face Charteris, 'Vasagar's been playing both ends against the middle. He fed us enough information to ensure that he was seen as one of the good guys, on the right, winning side. At the same time he did a deal with Flynn. He told you the dud notes were coming in on the boat — but then made sure the notes wouldn't be coming. Then, once he knew the operation was called off, he also knew the coast was clear to pick up the boat's new cargo. Not notes, but guns.'

'That reasoning seems tortuous to me. Do you have any information that he knew Flynn?' Charteris asked suspiciously.

'Vasagar knew about Cleaver. DS Start admits he gave us Cleaver's name. Can there be any doubt he knew about Flynn as well?'

'There's still a flaw in this, sir,' Elaine Start objected.

'Which is?'

'If we assume Vasagar was after the guns, how come we end up with two dead men on that boat? And the guns were still there. Why didn't Vasagar pick them up, after killing Flynn and Cleaver?'

Charlie stared at her, unwilling to give way, but recognising the logic in her questions. 'The whole thing went sour,' Charlie contended. 'In any case, we won't know what happened until we get our claws into Vasagar. My guess is it all started with Cleaver and Seamus Flynn, who I believe were partners in distributing counterfeit notes, now upping the stakes, running guns. Vasagar now had two problems, two operations muscling in on his territory. There's the possibility he'd approached Cleaver, threatened him, said he wanted a slice of the action over the guns, but then at the last moment the deal went sour — who the hell knows what makes villains fall out from time to time? I think something went badly wrong on that boat, and Vasagar had it put right.'

'If all this is true — and it's only supposition,' Charteris said quietly, 'I still can't see that Vasagar would have been personally involved.'

'DCI Spate has given us a description of the one man who left that boat,' Elaine Start announced crisply. 'As far as I can gather, the description does not fit Mark Vasagar. '

'Aw, come on, we all know Vasagar doesn't get personally involved as Mad Jack Tenby used to be in the old days! Vasagar would have employed a hitman,' Charlie argued. 'It would be his style. I saw two people get out of that car and go down to the boat. One of them would have been Cleaver. My guess is that Flynn would have got on the boat at Middlesbrough with a few crewmen, loaded the packing cases, stayed on board keeping an eye on the merchandise. He told the crew to get lost; I saw them heading for town. They were in a good mood and relaxed: they probably had no idea what was going to happen. Flynn stayed on the boat. He was waiting for his partner, and Vasagar's contact man, who was coming to inspect the goods, maybe. When they arrived . . .'

In his mind's eye he could recall the scene he had witnessed. The dark car, the two men leaving the car, crossing the yard, climbing aboard. And he remembered the sudden gust of wind, the gurgling of the rippling water breaking on the riverbank, odd plopping sounds. He had thought of those sounds as water lapping against the hull. He knew now it had been something else: a handgun, shots fired through a silenced muzzle.

'We don't know what made the thieves fall out,' Charlie said, 'but it's pretty clear that there was a serious disagreement. Maybe Flynn was trying to welsh on the deal; maybe the guns weren't what was ordered. I don't know. But the guy who went aboard with Cleaver was a professional. He took Cleaver out cleanly. He took more pleasure in finishing off Flynn. Maybe because Flynn was the one who caused the trouble.'

'You say this man then casually walked back to the car.'

'Because Vasagar had told him there'd be no police presence at the landing; he would have known the counterfeit note smuggling run had been called off after the raid at Monkwearmouth.'

'There's a hell of a lot of "maybes" in all this. But all we have to do,' Charteris remarked, 'is find out who Vasagar employed to do the killing. If, of course, Vasagar really was involved in the manner you suggest.' He leaned back in his chair, linked his fingers together and scowled at Charlie. 'All right,' he announced unwillingly, 'let's take a flyer on this. If Vasagar has been making a fool of us, let's take him down. DCI Spate, reluctantly, I'm taking you off suspension. I'm not overlooking your deliberate disobeying of instructions, nor the way in which you were abetted by DS Start. I've no doubt you pulled rank on her to achieve what you wanted.'

I wish, Charlie thought to himself.

'But I'm pulling you off suspension so you can follow up this . . . theory of yours. DS Start can hand over what's left to do on the counterfeiting liaison and work with you. I want results on this investigation, Spate. We're stalled on the killing of Dieter Barschel. I want a quick result on the murders of Flynn and Cleaver. And I don't want to see any more banner headlines in the Press. If Vasagar is involved, handle him carefully. You don't move on him until I get a full report. You hear what I say?'

'Sir.'

'Now get the hell out of here, both of you.'

They left smartly. Charlie was jubilant. In the corridor he turned, gave Elaine a high five. 'DS Start, we have something to celebrate. The Prince of Wales. Immediately. I'm pulling rank. That's an order.'

* * *

It was early and the bar was quiet. Charlie ordered a gin and tonic and a Famous Grouse. He carried them back to the table. 'Fond memories,' he said, and raised his glass in a toast. It was a pleasant surprise to him when she smiled.

'Are you really convinced about all that stuff you gave the ACC?' she queried doubtfully.

'Hey, it sounded good to me,' Charlie enthused.

She regarded him soberly. 'DCI Spate, you know you've got a thing about Mark Vasagar. You could be wrong about all this.'

'I could be right.'

'All I'm saying is, maybe we shouldn't jump too many hurdles too quickly on this one. Let's not assume too many things.'

'DS Start, the important thing is I'm back in harness. And yes, maybe I do have a thing on Vasagar and I want to nail him so much I'd give up anything to do it.' He eyed her lasciviously. 'Well, not *anything,*' he added.

She held his glance for several seconds, and then heaved a long sigh. She shook her head. 'This has been going on for far too long,' she muttered, almost to herself. She clucked her tongue in submission. 'Drink up, Charlie, it's time we got this sorted, once and for all.'

'How do you mean?' he asked, raising his eyebrows.

'The booze is cheaper at my place,' she said resignedly.

* * *

In the darkened room, Charlie turned over on his side. He could make out the bedside clock: three-thirty a.m. Beside him Elaine Start lay sprawled. He was aware of the warmth of her flesh; he recalled the urgency of her response to his passion; now, he could hear the light gurgling sound she made in her throat as she slept. He would never understand women. To Charlie Spate, would-be hedonist, women remained an enigma. He had laid siege to Elaine Start's virtue for two years; she had rejected his more clumsy advances; he had agonised over her indifference and, finally, he had confessed his sexual sins to her when he had visited her house. The consequence, as he saw it, was that she had thrown him out just as things had started to get interesting.

And now, when he hadn't even been trying, when he was simply crowing at his success in getting his suspension lifted, it was she who had made the suggestion. He would never understand women.

She turned, thrust her hip against him, murmured, 'What's the time?'

'Three-thirty.'

'Bloody hell . . .' She groped under the bedclothes. 'Will you never give over?'

Charlie hadn't even been thinking about it, but he was quite prepared to accept a challenge.

It was gone seven-thirty when he woke again. Groggily he sat up in bed. The result of the solid drinking in which they had indulged before collapsing in Elaine's bedroom had furred his tongue, left the roof of his mouth dry as sandpaper. Elaine stirred beside him, one arm flung out, the softness of her left breast exposed. She was half awake. 'Did the earth move for you, Charlie?' she murmured sleepily.

'Three times.'

'You do understand that this is just a one-off, don't you?'

'*Three* off,' he corrected her. 'You fancy a cup of tea?'

'Charlie, you can be magic.'

He suspected she was not referring to his sexual prowess. He padded downstairs, naked, to the kitchen. He reminded himself that in his state it was important not to spill boiling water. He filled the electric kettle, flicked it on and stood waiting, yawning, aware of the slight ache in his muscles. It had been a while. Even with Romy Arendt, it hadn't been as . . . physical. He wondered whether Elaine worked out at the gym. He must remember to ask her.

Romy Arendt. He wondered where she had got to. The story was, London. But what the hell . . .

There was a rattle at the front door. He peered around into the hallway. The morning paper lay on the floor inside the front door. *The Times.* He'd always known Elaine Start was a classy broad. He padded into the hallway, picked up the newspaper, and went back into the kitchen just as the rattling of the electric kettle reached a crescendo. They could share a teabag, he decided. Really domestic stuff. Newspaper under his arm, two mugs of hot tea in his hands, Charlie went back to the bedroom.

Characteristically for a woman, she seemed irritated when he shook her awake, gave her the mug of tea. He climbed in beside her; she sat up and there they were, side by side, in a situation he had dreamed of for two years, and there wasn't even a twitch where it mattered.

She sipped her tea. 'Charlie,' she said, 'I've been thinking.' That wasn't all she'd been doing. 'This fixation you've got on Vasagar. It's all very well, but do the facts really fit?'

'Close enough for me.' He shifted in the bed, his right leg moved closer, one naked ankle across hers.

'And you still haven't given Charteris all the information you've got.'

'Such as?'

'The stuff you told me about the East German death squad.'

'Aw, come on, Elaine. What's that got to do with Vasagar, and Cleaver, and Flynn, and counterfeiting and gun running—'

'And Dieter Barschel?'

He sighed. 'All right, I admit, his involvement is still a puzzle. Events seem to have sort of swirled around him.'

'Well, think a bit more about it, Charlie. We don't want this to turn into a wild goose chase, going after Vasagar.'

'Fat chance,' he disagreed. Slightly irritated, he picked up the newspaper, opened it to the sports page, found nothing of interest, then idly worked backwards through the newspaper.

'Why do men always do that?' she asked in wonder.

He hardly heard her. His attention had been caught by an item, a headline on page five. *'MYSTERY EXPLOSION'*.

He read the brief report. He slid his legs out of bed. He began to dress. Elaine watched him, puzzled. 'So is that it?' she asked with a hint of petulance. He ignored her, got his shoes on, headed for the bedroom door.

'There's something I got to check,' he explained hurriedly. 'I'll be in touch in an hour or so.'

He closed the front door behind him with a bang. It was pointless phoning the hospital — he'd just be given the run around. He was only a few minutes away, in any case. He started the engine of his car, drove away, swinging into the main road.

At the hospital he walked straight up to reception, showing his warrant card. 'You've got a patient by the name of Hannah Guderian. Which ward is she in?'

The blonde, middle-aged receptionist was flustered. She checked her computer records hastily. At last she looked up and said, 'She's been discharged.'

'How come? She'd been in a coma for days. She was just convalescing. She can't have been—' He hadn't been keeping in touch. 'Who picked her up?'

'I'm afraid I have no information on that,' the receptionist replied, almost in tears at his urgency.

Ward. It had to be Ward. Angry at himself, he stormed out of the building. He flicked on his mobile phone. He rang Ward's mobile number. There was no response. It had been switched off. He rang Ward's office on the Quayside. There was a short delay and then Susie Cartwright answered. She was breathing hard as though she was in a hurry.

'Where's your boss?' Spate demanded.

'Who is that? Your voice — is that DCI Spate?' Anger seeped into her tone. 'It's just eight o'clock, I've only just got in, haven't had time even to take off my coat—'

'To hell with your problems. Eric Ward will have picked up Hannah Guderian from the hospital,' Charlie snapped.

'That's right, but—'

'Where did he take her?'

Clearly flustered, Susie Cartwright said, 'Well, she was getting better it seems, but still needed rest, a quiet environment, so Mr Ward rang his ex-wife and she agreed that Miss Guderian could stay at Sedleigh Hall. What's this all about, Mr Spate?'

'Where is Ward now?'

'He had an interview with a client yesterday, up in Berwick. He told me he wouldn't be back in the office till this afternoon. It was easier to spend the night at Sedleigh Hall. Mr Spate, what is this about?'

There was no time to explain. He switched off his mobile, drove back to Elaine Start's house. He hammered on the door; she opened it, peered around at him. 'You've got a nerve—'

'Get dressed. We're heading north.'

He prowled around downstairs while she dressed. He tried Ward's mobile again, found it was still switched off, cursed, rang Susie Cartwright again. She was more composed now. 'What is it you want now?' she asked coolly when he identified himself.

'Sedleigh Hall. I didn't get the phone number from you.' He heard her sigh in exasperation. A brief delay, and then she gave him the number.

Elaine came downstairs. He hurried her to the car. 'You drive.' He tried the Sedleigh Hall number Susie Cartwright had given him.

Eric Ward answered.

CHAPTER 16

It was not often that Eric Ward went to Berwick. He liked the town; it had an air of dogged certainty about it, he felt, perhaps the result of the attention that had been bestowed upon it, having been fought over for centuries by the English and the Scots. It was a solid, square-set town that exuded a comfortable, middleclass air, grown fat on tourists who came to admire the bastions and the sixteenth-century gateway, to walk along the ramparts and enjoy the sharpness of the air, and wander along Sandgate or enjoy the scene presented by the open sea and the nets of the salmon fishers in the Tweed.

Eric's latest client was no tourist, though he had spent time in various parts of England as a resident of more than one of Her Majesty's establishments. But in his present dilemma he swore that he was innocent of all wrongdoing. In his soft, Scottish Lowland accent, he had earnestly explained matters to Eric, as he sat in the police cell with his hands linked between his knees.

'It was all about this wumman, you see, Mr Ward. I got this business partner, you know, we been trading in gold, all legitimate like, though there was a little problem a way back with VAT payments but that all got sorted out, but I wasn't best pleased with the way he'd been dealing and I went around to kind of remonstrate with him like and he wasn't in, and the wife asked me in and she sort of sympathised with me, and well, you know how one thing leads to another . . . Anyway, we was just about finished when my business partner comes home, don't he, and he slaps her around a bit while I get out of there, and that evening he comes around to my house and breaks a window. Now fair's fair, I go out there thinking it's burglars or something and I had this .22 . . .'

Eric had groaned at that point. It had been a tussle over a gun, the police had turned up, arrested both men for affray, and then the question of a licence for the gun arose.

'It's not even my gun,' his client had explained. 'It was his. The fact is, when I did a runner away from his house I took the .22. I mean, it was a matter of caution, you know; in the state he was in he could've used it on his wife — or me, for that matter. I was just acting in self-defence, and no one was hurt anyway, just a few tiles blown off a bluddy roof, so I don't know what all the fuss has been about . . .'

It was seven in the evening before Eric was able to make his escape. He rang Susie, told her he'd stay the night at Sedleigh Hall and be back in the office some time after lunch. Anne was happy enough to put him up; by the time he finally arrived at Sedleigh Hall Hannah had already gone to bed.

'How is she?' Eric had asked.

'She's fine,' Anne had replied breezily. 'She gets tired in the evening, and tends to go to bed early, but I think staying here is doing her a lot of good. She keeps apologising for the inconvenience she's causing, says she should get back to Germany but I've told her she's welcome to stay on until she's properly fit to travel. There are occasions when she becomes a bit introspective, but she hasn't said much about what's happened.' There had been a short pause. 'She speaks very warmly of you, Eric.'

There had been something in her tone that had made him glance at her, with a wry smile. 'I've told you before. This is just business, Anne.'

'I'm sure it is,' she had responded coolly.

'Does her memory seem to be coming back?' he asked.

'She's not talked much about that. It seems she still recalls nothing about the accident. But she's more relaxed; she's taken to going on walks by herself, up on the hill.' She looked at him steadily. 'Where you and I used to go, in the old days.'

He'd met her level gaze, and nodded. 'That all seems a long time ago.'

'Yes. A long time ago.'

They had a nightcap together before she showed him his room. The drive from Newcastle to Berwick and back had tired him; he slept heavily and it was almost nine o'clock before he rose. Anne was in the breakfast room, alone.

'Hannah still asleep?' he asked, yawning.

'Not as much as you are,' Anne replied with a smile. 'No, she's already had her breakfast and she's gone for a walk. She's quite taken with the exercise. And it's a bright, fine morning. I think she's gone up to Ravenscar Crag.'

'There aren't many better places to ride or walk.' Eric had a brief image in his mind of how it had used to be when he had first lived in Sedleigh Hall. He and Anne had just married and all the early days seemed to have been sunny, as he now recalled them. They had ridden along the forested trails, walked on the crags, lain on their backs in the sweet grass and watched the high hawks circle. And talked. They had talked a lot. He caught Anne looking at him quizzically, one eyebrow raised. He smiled. As they had agreed last night, it was all a long time ago.

The telephone shrilled. Anne was nearest and she picked up the receiver. After a moment she handed it to Eric, grimacing. 'He's short on manners. It's for you.'

The man's voice was snappish. 'Ward?' Surprised, Eric said, 'Yes. Who's that?'

'Charlie Spate.'

'You sound a bit . . . fuzzy.'

'I'm in the car. I've been trying to get hold of you. Your mobile's been switched off. Is the girl still with you? Hannah Guderian?'

He sounded almost incoherent. Puzzled, Eric said, 'Yes, she's here. Why? What's the matter?'

'Keep her under wraps. I'm on the way up; DS Start is driving me. We need to talk.'

'I don't understand. What's the urgency? What's happened?'

'You seen the paper this morning? You take *The Times*?'

'Well, yes,' Eric admitted. 'But I haven't had time to look—'

'No matter. We'll be there within the hour is my guess. I'll see you then, we can talk about it.'

'About what? I don't—'

The mushy noise increased and then the telephone went dead. Spate had rung off. Frowning, Eric handed the receiver back to his ex-wife. 'What's the matter?' she asked, concern in her voice.

Eric shrugged. 'The hell if I know. That was our old friend DCI Spate, as you might have gathered. He's on the way up here.'

The prospect clearly displeased her. 'What for?'

'I've no idea. Maybe there's been some developments . . . He mentioned *The Times*. Has it arrived this morning?'

'As usual,' she replied. 'Seven on the dot. Very reliable new paper boy; cycles up from the village. It's over there, on the kitchen table. I've already had a look at it, so you won't get it uncrumpled. Like me to run a hot iron over it? You used to like to be the first to read it.'

'Very funny.' Eric took the newspaper as she handed it across to him and sat down at the breakfast table. 'What the hell is Spate on about?'

He shook open the newspaper. There was nothing he could see on the front page that was of particular interest, nor on the second page. The third page was taken up with an account of a public enquiry into a bungled murder investigation in the West Midlands, but he could see nothing there that might concern himself or Hannah Guderian. He glanced briefly at page five and saw the report it held.

MYSTERY EXPLOSION

Contrary to earlier reports, the possibility that the explosion three days ago in Mill Road, London was the result of terrorist activity has now been discounted by the police. A spokesman today confirmed that the likelihood was that the damage had been caused by a faulty gas appliance which had ignited . . .

Eric lost interest and moved on, methodically scanning each page of the newspaper. It contained the usual run of news stories, trouble in Iraq, thoughts about Iran, a missing teenager, a leader on the National Health Service crisis, talks between senior officials from Britain and the USA. He could see nothing of concern, nothing he could imagine would have caused Charlie Spate to rush hotfoot up to Sedleigh Hall.

Then something slowly moved in his stomach, an awareness, the recollection of an address. Mill Road. Quickly he turned back to page five, switched his attention down the page.

. . . faulty gas appliance which had ignited. The explosion was fortunately confined to the ground floor and although tenants were advised not to return to the upper floors for the time being it would seem that no great structural damage had been inflicted. The Fire Service and Police were quickly on the scene and the small blaze that had begun was quickly brought under control. The dead man, who lived on the ground floor, was apparently in receipt of disability benefits. He has now been identified as a part-time journalist called Jacobsen . . .

Eric sat stiff-backed, staring at the words, his mind whirling. Jacobsen. Charlie Spate had seen the report, and his reaction had been immediate. Jacobsen . . . and Hannah Guderian.

'You said Hannah has gone for a walk?' Eric snapped. 'Where exactly? Do you know?'

Anne shook her head, her eyes widening at the urgency in his tone. 'I told you already: she usually goes up to Ravenscar Crags. But I don't know she's done so this morning. I mean, she didn't say. She often walks up through the copse; sometimes climbs up on the Crags. But precisely where she's gone on this occasion . . . what's the problem, Eric?'

He hesitated, biting his lip. He stood up, throwing the newspaper aside. 'I'd better go find her.'

His anxiety was communicated to her. She rose also, putting out a hand. 'I'll come with you.'

'No. Stay here. I'll go find her. She'll not be in any trouble, but I'd better bring her back here. You need to be here in case Spate arrives before I find her: you need to explain where I've gone.'

Anne wanted to argue but he forestalled her, walking quickly into the hallway, shrugging into a jacket and heading out of the front entrance. He stared about him: the clouds were high, streaks of blue appearing in long splinters, rose-edged, promising a fine day. He hesitated, looking about him: Hannah could be almost anywhere on the estate. He himself had walked with her through the woods and up into the meadow; but Anne had mentioned Ravenscar Crags, and there were other possibilities, many areas where she could wander. If he followed on foot, if he tried to find her by walking the fields it could be hours before he tracked her down. It would be quicker, easier if he was mounted. He turned, hurried down to the stables. Anne kept three horses; one of the stable boys was there now; grooming one of the animals. The boy assisted Eric in saddling the bay: Eric knew him well, a broad-chested stallion with plenty of fire in him. He swung up into the saddle and clattered out of the stable yard.

The stallion clearly had not been exercised recently; there was a spring and excitement in the animal's gait as Eric rode him across the meadow to the side of the house and into the rising slope of the hill. Perhaps some of the tension in Eric was communicated to the horse also; it snorted, pulled at the reins, eager to race across the lush grass, but Eric pulled him left, towards the copse of trees clumped at the side of the hill, where he would be able to obtain a view across the lower fields. The bay was still straining at the bit when Eric was riding past the trees and something caught his attention. He reined in. A half mile from the house there was a rough track leading up into the copse from the main road; something glinted darkly through the screening trees.

Eric turned the stallion, slowing, edging the animal towards the copse. At the edge of the trees he dismounted, tied the reins to a branch. The stallion snorted impatiently as Eric pushed his way through scrub and low bushes. He caught sight of the car, made his way towards it along the track. The big, dark-coloured Mercedes had been parked half hidden by the trees. The windows were tinted. Eric knew he had seen it before.

There was ice in his veins when he turned, hurried back through the trees and swung himself into the saddle. He jerked the animal's head around, and urged the stallion for the hill. It responded enthusiastically, nostrils flaring and muscles bunching as it lengthened its stride, raced into the lower slopes of the hill and then slowed, scrambling as Eric swung left, crashing through long grass and bushes, heedless of the danger provided by the inevitable rabbit holes on the slope. He had no idea where Hannah Guderian might have gone, but if he was to have any chance of finding her quickly the best opportunity would be if he could reach Ravenscar Crags. Anne had guessed it would be where Hannah was headed; equally important, from there Eric would have a panoramic view of the estate. He cursed as he rode, realising he should have stopped, picked up some binoculars but it was too late for that now. He felt the stallion's muscles gathering as they leapt a small burn; the track winding through the grass ahead of them twisted and turned and Eric leaned forward as the going became steeper. Grouse burst into the air in front of them, cackling protests; rabbits scurried away, white tails bouncing through the undergrowth, but Eric urged the snorting horse upwards into the steep slope.

When they finally reached the steep rise that took them to the crags themselves, the stallion was breathing hard. Eric slowed, allowed the animal to relax from its exertions, and they paced carefully up the final hill. Eric now had a good view of the estate lands spreading out behind him, and to both sides. He turned in the saddle, looking about him, taking in the meadows below, the distant copses, the ploughed fields away to his right, and the winding tracks among the heather where occasional deer roamed, but he caught sight of no human movement; he felt the first, dreaded scratching again at the back of his eyes, stress-induced pain, and he squeezed his lids tightly shut, willing the pain to subside, calming the thunder in his veins. This was no time to have an attack; no time to have to deal with the familiar old stabbing, scratching agonies.

He pulled up the stallion at the edge of the crags. In front of him stretched a wide panorama: fields, tumbling burns, meadows, distant slopes and far away, thirty miles as the crow flies, the placid blue of the sea. Anne and he had ridden up here often in the old days, but never with the kind of urgency that now gripped him.

He sat there in quiet desperation for almost a minute, staring about him. He felt the quivering of the animal's body as it awaited his next instruction, and then, just as he was about to turn away and head out across the rocky ridge, he saw her. A flood of relief surged through him as he caught sight of the moving figure, emerging from the copse through waist-high ferns and into the meadow below. She was moving slowly, clearly enjoying her surroundings, her face raised to the sun now breaking brightly through the thin clouds. She was there, she was safe, and he shook his head in relief, almost regretting the panic that had sent him up there.

But there was still the car, on the forest track.

The stallion snorted impatiently as Eric turned, pulling at the reins. They moved sideways and downwards, taking the perilous track down from the front of the crag towards the meadow; stones sliding and rattling down the slope until they reached one of the several grassy platforms that formed the hill below the crags. Here the going was easier; they crossed one platform, and took the looping trail that led further down. For a moment Hannah was out of sight, but a few seconds later Eric rounded the bend and he saw her again. She had one hand raised to her forehead, shading her eyes against the sun, as though she had caught sight of him on the crag. She was only just within calling distance, for the slopes would muffle his shouting, but there was no need to call, she had seen him, and she raised her other hand in a wave of welcome.

Then the stallion snorted in sudden fright, and danced sideways.

The big man was as startled as Eric. He could not have heard the sound of their descent from the crags, in spite of the rattling stones. Their approach over the springy grass of the platform had been soft, but Hannah's waving hand had warned him. He had turned from where he lay prone at the edge of the flat grassy area, half screened by fronds of fern, and for both of them it was as though time slowed, almost stood still. Eric's startled gaze locked with steel-grey eyes, and there was a pause that seemed endless. The big man in the grass was the first to react, overcome his surprise. He was turning, rolling, bringing up the thing he held in his hands, swinging the muzzle in Eric's direction.

Eric had time to register only that it was a rifle before almost instinctively he kicked his heels to the stallion's side and charged the man on the ground.

The intruder was not quick enough to bring the rifle to bear but he still managed to loose off one shot, wildly, into the air, before the stallion's shoulder took him heavily, as he was rising from his position, and he fell backwards, rolling, losing his grip of the rifle. The stallion stamped, excited breath whistling through its nostrils as Eric turned his head around; the man was on his knees, grabbing for the rifle again, and his hand was on its butt when Eric rode into him a second time. The horse whirled, kicking out in fright and excitement, and Eric momentarily lost control as the intruder cried out in agony and fell backwards away from the platform edge. Eric's charge had sent him twenty yards beyond the man in the grass; he wheeled the horse and rode back, swinging quickly down from the saddle, kicking the rifle aside. He ran to the edge of the platform; the stranger was some twenty feet below him, struggling, writhing among the ferns that clustered on the rocky slope. He was staring back up the hill at Eric, his grey eyes wide with panicked determination. Eric, scrambling down the slope towards him, had time to note that the man was wearing a belted camouflaged jacket, and his right hand was groping inside the jacket, almost helplessly. When Eric reached him he saw the grimace of pain, the agony that seemed to be racking the man and he knelt down beside him, roughly pulled at the jacket and grabbed the weapon the intruder had been straining to reach. The man's steel-grey eyes fastened on the hand gun; his mouth was twisted in pain, and Eric realised that he was in physical trouble. He seemed to be unable to coordinate his limbs; his hands were shaking, his face contorted in agony. When the stallion's shoulder had hit him he had fallen, he had been kicked in the back and chest before he rolled down the slope. Either the kicking, or the consequent fall, had incapacitated him. Eric guessed the man might even have suffered a broken back.

There was no sympathy in Eric's veins. 'Who the hell are you?' he ground out.

The man who had wanted to kill Hannah Guderian was a big man, with the mouth and eyes of a fanatic. He was in his mid-forties, grey hair cut in a severe stubble. Long, harsh experiences had cut deep lines in his face; in spite of pain now; and his inability to move, his vicious determination still shone through. He said nothing; a slow trickle of blood emerged from his mouth where he had bitten his lip in the fall. He would say nothing, Eric knew.

Eric stood up. He waved to Hannah and called her name. Slowly she ascended the slope as Eric sat and stared at the man who lay there, unable to move. A weakness stole through Eric's body: the adrenalin had ceased to pump and he was aware of a slight trembling in his hands as he held the hand gun, and stared woodenly at the injured stranger.

It was ten minutes before Hannah finally made it to the platform. Her eyes were wide in surprise as she saw the man lying in front of Eric. 'What's happened? Who is he?'

'I don't know. But he came up here to kill you,' Eric said flatly.

She began to shake. He took her hand and led her up to where the stallion waited. He mounted, gave Hannah a hand so she could swing up behind him. He glanced down at the injured killer below. He noted the occasional shudder that traversed the man's burly frame, the twisting of the legs, the arched back. He could take Hannah down now.

The man who had wanted to kill her wouldn't be going anywhere.

Hannah's arms were tight around him as they rode back down to Sedleigh Hall. Her face was buried against his back, and he could feel the trembling of her body.

'But who is he?' she asked. *Who is he?*

CHAPTER 17

There were flights ready to board to Milan, Majorca, Palma, and Rome. The Dublin flight had already departed. The bar at Newcastle Airport was busy; Charlie Spate was waiting there while Eric said goodbye at the departure gate to Hannah Guderian, on her way to Stansted to catch a connection to Munich.

In the last two weeks she had improved considerably in health and confidence. When Eric had brought her down from the crags she had been shaking, in considerable distress, and when Anne had taken her in her arms she had burst into tears. Here, at the airport she had been in control of herself. Eric went to shake hands with her, but she reached forward, kissed him lightly on the mouth. 'I owe you my life,' she said.

He smiled. 'I think you ought really to be thanking the horse.'

'I know where my gratitude lies. And now, after all that has happened, I feel it is time to lay things to rest. I have come to terms with the knowledge that Andrea will never come back; I will never find where her body lies, but at least one of the men responsible for her disappearance, now he will pay the penalty. For her, for poor Mr Jacobsen, and for all the others . . .'

As she headed for the departure gate and was lost to sight, Eric thought back to the Ravenstone Crags. He had brought Hannah Guderian down to Sedleigh Hall and dismounted, led her inside and DCI Spate had arrived with DS Start shortly afterwards. Anne had taken charge of the shaking Hannah while Eric led the police officers back up to the grassy platform below the crags. There was evidence of the fierce, dogged determination and hardness of the man who lay there: in spite of his injuries he had tried to move, drag himself away through the ferns, but the effort had exhausted him, and he had fainted from the pain of his broken back. There were marks in the sparse grass where his fingers had dug into the earth in his agonised effort to get away from the scene; his fingertips were torn and bloody. Standing over him, Eric had felt no pity for the man. He was a cold-hearted, merciless killer. There was no telling how many had suffered at his hands over the years.

Charlie Spate had called in an air ambulance and along with DS Start they had waited there in the sunshine until the paramedics arrived. It was two weeks ago but the images and sounds were still vivid in Eric's mind: the harsh breathing of the injured killer, the bright sunshine, the trampled grass, and finally the beating thunder of the helicopter rotors. But now, it was all over.

Eric joined Spate in the bar. He had been surprised that the police officer had decided to turn up; he had been even more surprised when Spate had had the sensitivity to leave Eric and Hannah alone for a few minutes.

'So she's off back to Germany, now,' Spate said. He gestured towards the drink he had placed opposite him. 'Whisky,' he said. 'Cheers you up after painful partings.'

Eric nodded, ignoring the jibe. 'She's going to be all right now, I guess. And it seems she's come to terms with what's happened, and come to accept that her search for her missing half-sister is over. It's clear that Andrea Witt is dead, and maybe we'll never know where her body lies.'

'Count on it,' Charlie agreed.

'And Hannah almost joined her.' He glanced curiously at Spate. 'Have you managed to discover his identity?'

'Our broken-backed friend? The guy you and that nag put in a wheelchair for life?' Charlie nodded. 'We certainly have. It's caused quite a rumpus in Berlin. We took his fingerprints, and his photograph, and sent them to Interpol. According to his passport back in his hotel, and the cards we found in his wallet, he's Carl Jurgen, chief executive of a haulage firm in Munich, with subsidiaries scattered throughout Western Europe and Germany. Big company. But when they looked for matching information in criminal records it turns out he's a man who disappeared fifteen years ago. He was a member of a Stasi death squad that Jacobsen told us about: he and a couple of others got out, took new identities, became respectable businessmen. The German police have raided the haulage firm — which it seems was used for arms smuggling among other things — and several arrests have been made, and they're hopeful of finding the rest of the miscreants. The hunt is now on in earnest, to haul in his colleagues, and take his company set-up apart. The man we spoke to in London, Jacobsen, was right. Andrea Witt was right. The German authorities are now looking for Auerbach and Vogel. The man in the wheelchair — his real identity is Wilhelm Eigendorf.'

'A former member of the Stasi.' Eric was silent for a little while. He sipped at the drink Spate had bought him. 'Why did Eigendorf want to kill Hannah Guderian?'

Charlie Spate grunted and shook his head. 'She was just the last link in a chain of events. She didn't know him, but he thought it best to take no chances. He wanted to eliminate all possibilities. She had been looking for Dieter Barschel, and had spoken with Jacobsen, and she was trying to find out what had happened to her half-sister. That was more than enough for him. He had decided to cover all his tracks. Things had got out of control, and he wasn't the man to allow that.' Charlie pursed his lips in thought. 'It all really began with Seamus Flynn.'

'What did he have to do with Eigendorf?'

'Flynn's been an activist in the IRA for years. As such, he'd made contacts. And he had guns to offer. He was aware, through his criminal connections, that Eigendorf— or Jurgen, as he was now known — wasn't just running a legitimate haulage business. He was using the company as cover for a number of activities, one of which was running arms into Sierra Leone, the Sudan, West Africa, hell, anywhere there was trouble. Seamus Flynn, renegade former IRA member, offered him arms that were supposed to be part of the decommissioning process under the peace agreement in Ireland. Carl Jurgen came over to Newcastle to undertake the negotiations.'

Charlie sipped his drink. 'Seamus Flynn had decided to use Toddy Cleaver as his local agent, probably because he had learned Cleaver already had a history of involvement with Irish criminals — a false currency distribution operation in Dublin. Flynn approached Eigendorf, who came to England, where he was introduced to Toddy Cleaver, who'd be handling the local end of things in the north. The idea was that the arms would come in to Tyneside, then be shipped across to their eventual destinations by Carl Jurgen's haulage company. Unfortunately, during his little chats with Cleaver and Flynn, one of Cleaver's employees walked in. It was Dieter Barschel, who'd been running for Cleaver in his counterfeiting seam. Barschel and Jurgen — or Eigendorf as he now called himself— came face to face. Maybe Jurgen saw something in Barschel's eyes: he would have been sensitive to these things. It could have been puzzlement, at first; maybe a dawning recognition. Who knows? Immediate recognition was unlikely, after the years; it probably took Barschel a while to make the connection, but eventually Barschel remembered his old days with Dynamo Berlin, when he'd worked as an informer for the Stasi. He recognised his old colleague, masquerading as Carl Jurgen, and could put a name to him — Eigendorf.'

He grimaced, looked at Eric, shook his head again. 'Your informants, hey, they're pretty good but they didn't know the whole story. That Calico Jim, he misled us a bit.'

'How do you mean?'

'He told us Flynn and Cleaver were partners in the counterfeiting distribution. Fact is, Seamus Flynn was *never* involved in the counterfeiting business with Toddy Cleaver. They were linked only when Flynn, learning of Cleaver's Irish connections in Dublin, approached Cleaver about doing a deal with the guns. He wanted Cleaver's local knowledge and contacts: Cleaver agreed because he saw it as a way into the big time. But our German friend Eigendorf wasn't so sure about Cleaver — and when he knew he'd been recognised by Dieter Barschel, it looks as though he gave Cleaver a task. A sort of earnest of good faith, before he'd agree to deal with him and Flynn over the guns.'

'Get rid of Barschel,' Eric remarked slowly.

'Absolutely.' Spate hesitated, toying with his glass. 'But the trouble was, it looks as though Cleaver wasn't hard enough, or didn't get the message in the way it was meant. He decided to get Barschel put away by the boys in blue.' He clucked his tongue. 'This isn't just guesswork. We've finally traced that slut . . . Romy Arendt. Hiding out in Amsterdam. And she's confirmed it *was* Cleaver who paid her to arrange Barschel's arrest. She did it through me.' He glanced at Eric and scowled. 'You screwed me there, Ward, and I haven't forgotten it.'

Eric met his glance steadily, but made no reply.

'Anyway, Cleaver had made a mistake; putting Barschel away wasn't what Eigendorf had had in mind. They did things differently in the days he was in the death squad. And he was getting edgy about the whole arrangement over the arms deal. He felt exposed: he didn't rate Cleaver, was doubtful about him, and he'd been recognised by Barschel. Now, he felt he couldn't just walk away. So he left things to Cleaver and waited to see what would happen. But things got worse: you got Barschel out on bail.'

Eric nodded. 'When he came out, and I found him a haven, he was angry, but wouldn't tell me what it was about.'

Charlie Spate grunted. 'It's my guess that when Barschel recognised Eigendorf, he decided to do nothing about it. But when he found himself on trial, that was different. And he had a shot in his locker. The Stasi days had all been a long time ago, but when Barschel came west he'd brought with him papers that he thought one day might be useful. Details of the Stasi organisation he'd worked for. It was a sort of insurance. Barschel was livid about the way he'd been set up, and he had something to trade — the documentation he held could back up his identification of Eigendorf. We don't know whether he wanted to use the material just to warn Eigendorf to back off, or maybe he was stupid enough to think he could get away with blackmailing Eigendorf.'

'He contacted Cleaver?'

Charlie grimaced. 'Right. And he put some kind of proposition to him about the papers he had in his suitcase. That's when our Stasi friend decided it was best to deal with Dieter Barschel himself. We don't know whether it was Cleaver or Flynn who went with Eigendorf to the cottage—'

'How did they know I'd taken my client there after we got him bail?' Eric asked.

'Barschel was too long out of East Germany. He'd forgotten how hard these guys are. You told me he was angry; said he had something to do. Well, it looks like he phoned Cleaver; told him he had information on the man Toddy was dealing with — stuff he still kept in a case — and he'd sell it for the right kind of money. Bad mistake.'

'Information on Eigendorf's involvement with the death squad?'

'Right. It was stupid, and he paid for it. Eigendorf had a history, and he wasn't about to have a little man like Barschel cause him pain. It was easily enough done. A shotgun blast. They took the suitcase — we'll never know precisely what documents were in there, but they would have been damaging — and Eigendorf took Barschel's mobile phone too, so that the call to Cleaver couldn't be traced.'

'And Hannah Guderian?'

'It seems as though Eigendorf stayed in the vicinity of the cottage, keeping an eye on things, checking on developments. You reckoned yourself you might even have seen his car up there. He saw you arrive; saw you take the woman away to Stanhope. He knew about her relationship with Andrea Witt; he guessed she wanted to see Barschel, and he'd stopped that, but she was still another loose cannon in his life. He waited outside the hotel — then ran her down. Bad luck for him that he failed to kill her.'

'That's why he tried again later,' Eric surmised.

'That's so. But he'd realised before then that things were really unravelling; it was all getting too messy and dangerous for him. He was cooling on his negotiations with Flynn and he knew he was in jeopardy. Suddenly, there were too many loose ends, and too many risks to face. He should never have come to England in the first place; he should never have started negotiating with Seamus Flynn. So he geared himself to act as he had acted in his death squad days. First, he dealt with Dieter Barschel. Then Hannah at Stanhope. After that, to clean up the whole mess he had to go down to London. There was an old journalist enemy to get rid of — Jacobsen, who had directed Hannah to Barschel. The explosion in the apartment in Mill Road was no accident.'

'And he then returned to Newcastle?'

Charlie Spate nodded. 'He was thoroughly disenchanted with the arms deal. Dealing with Flynn and Cleaver had been a mistake. It was time to draw a line under the whole thing. The shipment was due in, but he was no longer interested. But he had to tie up the loose ends. He picked up Cleaver and drove to meet Flynn on the boat, ostensibly to see specimens of the merchandise, and to reach a final agreement. Then he did what he had been trained to do all those years ago. He put a bullet in Cleaver. With Flynn, he exacted a little revenge: I think he must have felt it was Flynn who was to blame for the mess — he should have arranged things with someone more competent than Cleaver. So he shot Flynn in the throat, let him die slowly, choking on his own blood.'

'You saw them on the boat?' Eric asked.

'I saw Cleaver and Eigendorf arrive; I saw Eigendorf leave. I couldn't make out what he was carrying. Now we know. It was one of the rifles: an Army issue SA8O. But he wasn't taking it as a souvenir. It was to be used to remove the last piece on his chessboard, Hannah Guderian, so that he could go back to Germany free from anxiety.'

'We — that is, Anne and I — had no idea he was in the vicinity. We thought Hannah would be safe at Sedleigh Hall.'

Charlie shook his head. 'This guy's done the rounds; he's a professional. It wasn't difficult for him. I've been talking to the hospital: it looks as though he checked with them, told them he was an uncle, and asked where she had been taken. They were quite accommodating: they said Mr Eric Ward had taken her to Sedleigh Hall. After that, it was a matter of stalking, checking out the location, waiting for an opportunity. I think he would have enjoyed that little cat and mouse game. But . . . well, he waited just a little too long.'

Eric leaned back in his chair. 'You can prove all this?' he asked.

'Typical of a lawyer,' Charlie jeered. 'Prove it? Hell, no. Eigendorf isn't coughing up much: he's a hard case and will stay silent until he thinks he can cut some sort of deal, even if he is crippled for life. Fat chance. No, a lot of it is guesswork, but it fits.'

ACC Charteris had asked the same question, and then added his comment. 'Your guesswork isn't all you crack it up to be, Spate,' he had sneered.

Defensively, Charlie had replied, 'All right, sir, I was wrong about Flynn and Cleaver being partners in the counterfeiting and about Vasagar holding back the delivery of notes in favour of the guns. The two activities were never connected. It's clear now that Vasagar didn't even *know* about the guns, but then, it was *your* own contacts in Cleveland who cocked that one up. It was *they* who'd first suggested there'd be a shipment of notes to Morden Landing when customs told them about suspicious boat movements on the Tees, when it was really guns — and when they discovered there were no notes to be sent to the Tyne it was they who moved in prematurely on the counterfeiters, leaving the shipment to run free!'

Charteris hadn't liked the implied criticism. And he was still sore at Inspector Martin's failure to make progress on the killing of Dieter Barschel. But Charlie had pointed to the fact they had the so-called Wilhelm Eigendorf, *alias* Carl Jurgen, on an attempted murder charge; Interpol had now confirmed the man's identity as, in reality, a hunted Stasi death squad member; forensic tests had demonstrated that the handgun used to kill Cleaver and Flynn was the same weapon that Eigendorf had tried to pull out of his jacket when knocked down by Eric Ward's stallion, and the rifle in his possession was from the same packing case as others found on the boat. And they'd found a fibre match at the cottage, from Eigendorf's clothing. 'It all *fits*,' Charlie had insisted.

* * *

'Yeah, we can tie it all in well enough.' Charlie glanced at Eric Ward. 'Besides, what does it matter? It means we can hang two murders and an attempted murder on Eigendorf, and I've no doubt if he ever survives a British term of imprisonment he'll then be extradited — still in his wheelchair, the doctors say. He's not going to be doing much by way of criminal activity in the future. We can't prove he killed Barschel, but we can prove from forensic tests on his car — that he was at the cottage, and that it was he who ran down Hannah Guderian at Stanhope, so the suppositions are reasonable. Forensic tests may come up with something in relation to the explosion that killed Jacobsen, but we'll see.'

He finished his drink, and rose to his feet, looking down on Eric. 'Anyway, you've seen off your little German girlfriend, safe and sound. And it looks as though it's all wrapped up. Except for one thing. It's why I came out to the airport, really.'

Warily, Eric asked, 'And what's that?'

'The thing between you and me. The way you stripped me bare in the courtroom. In view of what's happened, the top brass have let me off the hook, but I know damn well I'm on probation, got to keep my nose clean. Otherwise, I might be tempted . . . Anyway, the fact is, our little . . . cooperation can be regarded as at an end.'

'I can live with that,' Eric said in an even tone.

'I'm damn sure you can. But just you remember, Ward. I'm not a man who forgets.'

As he moved past Eric and headed towards the entrance Eric turned to watch him and remarked, 'I can still hardly believe it — one man causing such mayhem.'

Over his shoulder Charlie Spate said, 'Eigendorf? Believe it. It came naturally to him. He'd been a member of a death squad.'

THE END

ALSO BY ROY LEWIS

ERIC WARD MYSTERIES

INSPECTOR JOHN CROW

Don't miss the latest Roy Lewis release,
join our mailing list:

www.joffebooks.com

FREE KINDLE BOOKS

Printed in Great Britain
by Amazon

58278278R00123